GREGORY EL HARVEY

DRAGONS

IN

LOVE

A NOVEL

Books by Gregory El Harvey

JACKSONVILLE

Autobiographical
FACES IN THE SHADOWS

Serial
THE PATTERN OF A SNOWFLAKE
DRAGONS MORE DECENT THAN MEN
DRAGONS IN LOVE
TO DIE IN THE COLDEST WINTER
THE AUTONOMOUS ASSASSINS

Cover painting: *Dragons In Love* by Gregory El Harvey (www.gregharveygallery.com)

To Jinlong, my best friend,
who faithfully stood guard
during the writing of this book.

ACKNOWLEDGMENTS

I am grateful to Myanna Harvey for critically reading the manuscript and to Cassia Harvey for helping with the publication process.

CHAPTER 1

Carlysle, Pennsylvania, Summer 2010

Gretchin Wheeler stood beside the yellow car, her eyes fixed upon its owner as he joked with another presenter. Then she began to move around the car, occasionally giving her cup of ice and tea a vigorous shake. Stopping to look keenly at the car's grill, she removed the lid and straw and leisurely took a little of the ice with the tea. Replacing the lid and straw, she shook the cup again and continued to move around the car. This kind of theater had always been fun. Today, it was business.

"Hey there," he said to her after breaking off his conversation with the other man.

She had heard the tone before, not from him, of course, for that was why she was there, to meet him, to hear him, to engage him. In her youth she heard the tone often, in the voices of boys and then men who looked at her, longed for her, drooled after her. Now, in her fifties, she heard the tone less often, but still she heard it. In her youth, it would reach inside her every time she heard it, and even now she felt its pull. But today, on this particular day, she would deny the power, harness it, and put it to use.

He took a step closer, eyeing the bright-green blouse, the white skirt, the legs. "Like 'er?"

She removed her sunglasses, then lifted her eyebrows flirtatiously. "Sure. It's a pretty car. I like sports cars." And she watched as his eyes skimmed her cleavage.

"For a fact. Well, I do, too. That's why I'm here at the show. D'you know what this car is?"

"No," she answered, tossing her head to make her hair burst out in the sunlight. She watched his eyes jump to her hair, and she could see that he nearly choked.

"Well," he said, swallowing, "it's an Austin-Healey 100. It's got original seats, original wires, everything original. Except the top, had it cut myself. Great fit, don't you think?"

"Sure."

"Extremely well cared for. For a fact."

She met briefly his gleaming, greedy eyes as she sidled away from him to walk around the car. As every woman does, she knew what to do with her ass.

"You like yella?" he queried, following her.

"Yes," she cooed, "yellow is beautiful, sensuous. It's one of my favorite colors." She smiled innocently as he seemed unable to speak.

Momentarily he asked, "Did you ever ride in a Healey?"

"Not really." Delicately she ran a finger along the canvas top. She let her eyes move admiringly over the car's body, then looked up at him, straight into his eyes, and offered another smile.

Pulling the door open, he asked, "Wanna sit inside?"

She gave the cup a double shake. "Actually," she said, cocking her head to expose more of the dragon on her neck, "I'd like to go for a ride in it. Don't know if I'd be able to drive it. It's a beautiful car, but it looks like it'd be more than I could handle."

"I could take you for a spin, if you want, soon as the show's over. Wanna go?"

She lifted her shoulders briefly, "Where? Just around here?"

His mouth widened. "Sure, anywhere you want. I'll take you out on the road, if you want."

"Well," she said, "maybe." She gave the tattoo a delicate scratch, shook the cup, and closed her lips around the straw.

"We could even go right now. I could just take you around here. Come on."

She looked at him, as though she had never seen him before and didn't know whether to trust him. "Okay," she replied at length, her tone reluctant. "I'll have to call my dad. He's here at the show. Just to let him know. He's in his seventies, and I don't want him to worry."

"Of course, yeah, sure. Take your time. I'll start her up."

With the bounce of a school boy, he clambered in behind the wheel and pulled his door shut. He turned the key, waited for the fuel pump to finish, then pushed the starter button on the dash. His eyes followed her legs as she stepped aside to make the call.

"Daddy?" she said sweetly into the phone. "Listen, I'm going to take a ride with someone here in one of the cars. Just keep heading toward the British cars, and I'll be back before you get here. Okay? . . . Sure, sure. . . . Okay. . . . You've got your water bottle? Now, I want you to drink it. Don't get sunstroke. And keep your hat on. . . . See you then."

He had cracked her door. She pulled it open and climbed in. Tidily she smoothed the white skirt around her legs as she nestled into the bucket seat. The hem rose to a few inches above her knees, which she kept together. She was glad she had not agreed to the kydex and could close her legs.

"You won't need the seatbelt," he said, his eyes on her legs. "We're just goin' around here. Law makes you put 'em in, though, just to drive it here. I go to all the shows. Gotta have seatbelts, give me a break. Law's a buncha shit, isn't it?"

"Wow, it's close in here, and everything's so cute. Not a lot of room to move around, is there?"

"Not supposed to be. Feel how it's real down on the ground? And no windows, see that? They're in the trunk, the boot, that's British. They fit in those holes in the door. Hey, feel that engine? It's a nasty little four."

"What year is this?"

"Fifty-five," he answered proudly, pushing the stick to the far right, so that his hand touched her leg. Then he backed up carefully until he could clear the TR3 next to his space, lifted the stick and pulled it into first, and then let out the clutch.

"Whew," she said, grabbing the chromed handle on the dash. "Bumpy. It feels like we're on the ground."

"That's what I said, yeah. But you'll get it, don't worry. There's not much clearance. I'll keep it slow, don't wanna scare you. And I can't throw up any gravel, either. These guys've got a lot of money in their paint. Look at that Jag. One-fifty. Shit, he wouldn't trade a wheel for this car."

Moments later, beyond the last row of cars, he turned onto the highway and slowly brought the car up to speed.

"It's just a four, but it's hot." he said as the wind began to muffle his voice. "It's got electric overdrive in second and third. It feels great, doesn't it?"

As he went on about the engine, the transmission, the differential, the wire wheels, she made no attempt at a response, except an occasional perfunctory nod and smile. She could only think of Stanley's last words, *make it three or maybe all five, but then you are empty.* Life was like that, it always seemed simple to other people. Simple problems, simple answers.

They had not gone far from the exhibition area, when he turned onto a gravel road and drove between two corn fields. Pushing the stick into second, he gave a chuckle, like a kid playing with the gears on his bike.

"Sometimes you've gotta double clutch this car," he said, reducing their speed. "Know what double clutching is?"

"I've heard about it. But I'm not an expert, at all. It's like gear ratios, right?"

Gleefully he replied, "Not exactly, I'm afraid not. Normally you would push the clutch in once to shift out of one gear and into the next. Double clutching is where you push the clutch in to pull it out of one gear, but then let it out and push it in again to push it into the next gear."

"Oh, wow. And why would you do that?"

He smiled confidently. "Cuts down on grinding when going into the next gear. Some transmissions, especially older ones, grind. The newer transmissions have what's called synchromesh, so you don't need to double clutch. Got it? Think you can digest all that?"

Instead of replying, she queried innocently, her eyes upon the cornfields, "So, where is this?"

"Oh, I'm just going to go up here and turn around. . . . Then we'll go back. . . . That okay?"

"Okay, thanks," she replied. "Is this a farm?"

"No, there's a lake up here."

A minute later he pushed the stick into second, then first, and then braked.

"I don't see a lake," she said, looking around curiously. "Where's the lake?"

"Oh, it's up there. We'll have to walk a little. . . . Say, listen, let's just sit for awhile and talk. That okay?"

"Sure, I guess so."

He could not refrain from talking about the car, and again he told her about the folding windshield and the leather seats.

After listening patiently, she asked, "You sure this isn't a farm?"

"No, I've been out here before. There's nobody out here. Just us."

The field birds seemed to be calling to each other, and the sun shone golden and bright upon the corn tops. The sky was cerulean and clear.

When he put his hand on her leg and left it there, she turned to him and said softly, "Are you going to kiss me?"

He stared into her face, his eyes incredulous, then answered, "Yeah, . . . yeah."

"Wait," she breathed before their lips touched, "I brought something."

"Yeah?" he stammered.

"Yes," she replied, riveting her gaze on his eyes, "you know, for protection."

His eyes grew. "Sure, yeah."

Innocently she reached down into her purse, her eyes still fixed upon his, and enclosed the grip of the .38. Then, her lips parting sensually, her breath on his, she yanked up the gun, jammed it into his side and pulled its trigger twice—*Blam! Blam!*

"Ah-h!" he yelled, with a convulsing leap in his seat, his eyes instantly going shut and his whole face puffing into a mask of wretched pain.

Instantly she thrust the muzzle into his neck and fired again—*Blot!* The revolver's blast whacked his head to the side, where it hung halfway out the open window and over the door. Then, her heart pounding ferociously, she stretched her arm out, put the muzzle to just below his ear, and pulled the trigger again—*Schlop!*

She stared at him for only a moment, then calmly slipped the gun back into the purse holster. With a shaking hand, she rummaged through the purse for a tissue, withdrew it, wiped her nose and thrust it back into the purse. Then she reached back into the purse and found her phone.

"Bradley? ... Yes. ... I think it's about the second road on your left, no marker, between two cornfields. ... Yes. ... Just hurry, would you, I've got blood all over me. It's on my face, I think. God, what a mess! ... Wait, I can't get out. ... No, I meanit, I can't get out of the car. I can't find the latch. Stupid car! ... He said it was a '55 Healey or something. ... In the door? God, yeah, I've got it, okay, I've got it, I see it. Just get here."

She dropped the phone into the purse, reached into the door well for the cord, pulled it, and thrust the door open.

Her legs seemed unsteady as she walked around to the driver's side to wait for Bradley. Although she thought she might hear the approach of the Corvette's tires, she could only hear the birds calling over the cornfields. For a moment, she fixed her gaze down the road, but then ventured a glance back at the man. His head hung out over the door edge, as if part of a display in a museum of medieval executions. His eyes were closed. Blood ran in ghastly lines down the side of the yellow door and was collecting on the roadside gravel and grass. Then she looked up to see the Corvette and Bradley coming for her.

A brighter yellow, she thought, and no blood. Just paint, clean, shiny paint, and no dripping blood. God, what awful stuff oozes from human beings.

"Gracious, you're a mess," he exclaimed softly as she got in. "Look at you, you're covered with it.

You were supposed to shoot him, not butcher him."

Without responding, she pulled her door closed, then turned to stare at him, her eyes swimming with anger at his insensitivity.

"Don't get it on my car," he said. "Don't wiggle, Gretchin. Just sit there. Good grief, what a slob job. You're filthy. You need a shower. Good Lord, you need a bath. Don't touch anything, okay?"

"I won't," she replied softly, huddling down into the seat.

Turning the car around, he said, "My goodness, look at the blood on that door, and look at his head, like a pumpkin. Boy, that's some car." Then as he accelerated, he added, "That was a beautiful Healey. The car was worth more than the man, I think."

"What do you mean, *was*?" she blurted. "What the hell's wrong with you? The car can be washed, Bradley."

"Blood and meat? I don't think so. It would be like washing down a slaughterhouse."

"Thanks, Bradley. Thanks for being positive, helping me, encouraging me emotionally, you know, all that shit that normally a coworker might want to do. Yeah, just thanks one hell of a lot, stooge. God!"

At the inn he eased the Corvette around back and pulled in beside the team's gray SUV. Shutting the engine down, he looked at her again, then got out.

Martina opened the suite door for them, then closed it quickly behind them. At first, she was silent, as if in unbelief. Although as team leader she had seen much blood spatter on colleagues, she had not seen so much flesh in the mix.

Once inside, Gretchin turned around, as if to present herself. Her face, the front and left side of her hair, the blouse, the skirt, even her legs, were covered with specks of blood and particles of flesh. "I'm a mess, I know, but I got the guy, I really got him."

Martina, her mouth slightly open, made a face of disgust at the sight, then said, "What in the world did you do, blow his head off?"

"I don't know. Maybe I hit the jugular, I don't know."

"Oh, his head was still on," said Bradley, hanging his hat on the corner of a chair. "Awful mess running down that car door. How to ruin an Austin-Healey in one easy step, I think."

Gretchin threw him a stare. "Don't start, just don't start."

Martina reached to put a hand on the bloodied shoulder, then refrained. "Why don't you run in and take a shower. Go ahead, go on. And it seems to be in your hair, a lot, I think, yeah."

When they could hear the shower running, she got him a soda from the fridge. "What are you listening to, Bradley? She's taking a shower. You know, no clothes. Can't you handle that?"

"Of course. Don't be crass, Martina."

She grabbed the hat and tossed it to him. "Just go back to your room. I'll call you when she's out. And bring one of the trash bags." Then she muttered, "Why would you wear a white skirt to shoot a man point blank in a small car?"

As she waited for him to pull on the hat, slurp the soda, as she knew he would, and leave she grew annoyed at her impatience. When he was gone, she sat on the bed and rubbed her forehead. But she should not need to do that, she thought. The team leader should not need to massage her forehead. Then the bathroom door opened and Gretchin came out in her robe, her hair wrapped in a towel.

Taking the bundle of clothes, Martina queried, "How are you doing?"

A heavy blink. "I'm okay, thanks."

"Did he touch you?"

"Bradley?"

"No. The man."

"Oh. Well, let's just say, I touched him before he touched me. . . . No, he didn't touch me."

"That's good. These creeps stick it in every keyhole they find, and you don't want him sticking it in you."

"I know that, Martina. You don't have to tell me that. I'm fifty-five, for God's sake, you know that. You're not my mother, so don't say stupid things."

"I know, you're right. I'm just saying—"

"What are you saying?"

"Not a thing."

"But what is it with you, Martina? You're older, so you have to be ancient? Give me a break. I've got a lot on my mind, a lot more than worrying about some guy's dirty crank."

"Okay, okay, stop. I didn't mean it. I withdraw my concern. Just calm down. Would you like something to drink, a cold soda or something? We have to leave soon. You'd better get dressed."

CHAPTER 2

Lancaster County, Pennsylvania

Within the hour, the team were making their way back to Lancaster County. In the SUV, Stanley drove, Martina navigated, and Maggie sat behind with Gretchin. Bradley kept his distance as he followed them in the Corvette.

Darkening clouds, blown down from the Allegheny range to the northwest, soon began to drop their rain upon the peaceful landscape and turn the highway into a smear of tarry black. In short order the two vehicles' wipers went into action and their headlights came on.

"We did not beat it," said Stanley, his Russian accent thick.

Martina flipped her mirror up. "No, I didn't think we would."

From the back seat, Maggie offered, "The farmers will be happy."

"Yes," he chuckled. "It is said the same way in Russia."

As the cars rolled through the Estate's stone gateway and approached the larger of the old houses the rain slackened, but Martina still retrieved her umbrella and felt for its button.

Her husband smiled, switching the wipers off. "You are getting soft," he teased.

"No," she replied, "I'm just getting old."

Cracking her door, then pushing it open, Gretchin, who had been quiet during the trip, said coldly, "Sometimes I think you are, Martina." Then she got out, herself with no umbrella, and stood in the light rain.

The Russian also got out. "I will bring your things in, Gretchin. Do not get wet, just go in."

She did not respond to this, but only looked at him. She watched Martina get out and put up her umbrella. But Stanley's blue eyes pierced her, so that finally she apologized to Martina and got under her umbrella. She was glad when Martina said it didn't matter and pulled her close.

It was not until later, when the team had finished dinner and Bobbie Lee had served out slices of steaming pie and placed a pot of coffee on the table, that Gretchin began to feel normal again. But then, what was normal anymore, she wondered, pressing the side of her fork down through the pie.

"Like I've told y'all before," said Bobbie Lee, her accent tinged with Tennessee twang, taking her place at the table, "nobody has to eat my pie, but I'm takin' your name down if you don't."

Connors groaned, "I know what you're sayin', but I'm nowt lestenin'. I've put foive pounds on by eatin' your freggin' pies."

Bobbie Lee Henry merely smiled and poured herself a cup of coffee. She had never taken her pie without coffee and never would. And anyway, she liked this Kelly Connors, this Irish enigma with colorless eyes, nearly luminescent blond hair, and profane speech. She herself, from the hill country of what she liked to call the old Confederate South, could be a bit profane at times. But this woman from Cork—God, what a sewer her mouth could be.

Lifting her fork, she took a bite of the pie and placidly chewed, looking around the square table at the rest of the team. She liked them all really, even the cocky ex-public school principal Bradley Hopkins. Gretchin Wheeler, who had taught art at his school and who now seemed to scrap with him incessantly, could be very nasty and in your face. But yeah, she liked her for speaking her mind. Margaret Swift-Jones, the hoity-toity one, who had taught history at the same school, was considered pretty much the team's peace maker. Stanley Osipov, the Russian photographer who had worked with the old KGB, was hard for anyone to figure out. From his American cowboy boots to his extensive knowledge of the noir world, he seemed always just beyond the grasp of those who would understand him, define him. His wife Martina Jung Osipov, who had taught English, also at Bradley's school, was the team leader. She could be diplomatic or not, but was always dependable. The two hardened professionals, Connors and Packard, she admired immensely. If the former could be taken as nearly pathologically profane, the latter, this grayed and grisly Leonard Packard, could be taken as just plain pathological. But he knew his guns and how to use them. She herself, recruited from her ad hoc work with the Memphis police, had been the last addition to the team. Kessler had hand picked her to be the team's third professional. Stretching her arms and flexing her muscles, she gave her hair a swipe and grabbed her coffee again. Yes, she liked these people.

Fixing her gaze on Maggie, she queried, "How's that there tea?"

Maggie just touched the cup to its saucer. "It's very good."

"You're sure not keen on the coffee, are you?"

"No, no, I'm not," replied Maggie, a twinkle in her eyes. "Thank you for making the tea. And the rest of the meal was delicious, too. Many thanks from all of us."

"Yeah," agreed Bradley, "it was super good. Keep it up."

Gretchin shot him a look of disgust.

Then Maggie cleared her throat gently and asked, "Gretchin, I don't mean to be insensitive, but . . . how are you doing?"

The general low chatter and mealtime noise suddenly fell off as Gretchin's response was anticipated. Only Connors and Packard seemed indifferent.

Gretchin, who did not respond immediately, eventually looked up from her pie. "I'm actually fine," she said timorously. "At least, I think I am. But thanks, Maggie."

"I didn't mean to be—"

"I know, Maggie. It's all right. Thanks for asking. . . . I can talk about it, if you like." And lifting her cup, she sipped her coffee.

Bradley, directly across from her, gave the table a little slap. "Now, that is spirit. I think that's a great response. What more could anyone ask?"

Slowly she looked up at him, her eyes narrowing. "Hey, prick," she said as he grinned at her, "I thought you could only talk with food in your mouth."

Continuing to grin, he said nothing to this. Long experience in dealing with her had taught him that often the best way to defend against her vitriol was simply to grin at her but remain silent.

Stanley, his accent heavy, offered, "I am thinking that Gretchin has done the marvelous thing. It is not easy to do a job like this alone. It was her first time like this."

"I agree, Osipov," Bradley chirped. "I simply want to know if what I said was true." With this, he lifted his water glass and drank, his eyes upon Gretchin. He loved pushing her. If he spent a year of his life, he could not repay the aggravation she had given him. Oh yeah, she's vulnerable, he thought, just look at her cringing there. Now is the time to strike, give her back even a little of the misery he had experienced from the acid of her tongue.

Glaring, she replied, "Yes, it worked. Obviously, it worked. It worked, child, it fucking worked, okay? You're such an obnoxious little kid that you just couldn't wait to ask about the gun. So, yes, it worked. All right?"

"Oh, I know it worked," he chortled, his eyes darting. "You all should've seen this guy's head hanging out the window of his goofy sports car. You bet it worked. I told you, Gretchin, and I simply want to hear you admit it, a revolver is better than an auto in a close-up fight. Admit it, just admit it."

"Yes," she returned, her eyes growing larger, "it worked."

"Better," he persisted. "Say it worked better, please."

Pointing both forefingers at him, she spat out, "Asshole! What's the matter with you? I had to kill a man today."

"So, you're complaining?"

"No!" she shouted. "But I had to shoot him in the head, Mr. Bradley dick Hopkins, and you're getting all giggly about what gun I used, for God's sake? What are you, a fucking ghoul?"

Packard, swallowing a mouthful of pie, rasped, "I have to agree with Bradley about the gun. You wanna play with your junk, go ahead. But if you want it to work, get a wheel gun."

"Hey," piped Bradley loudly, "Gretchin Wheeler. Man, is that good?"

Giving him a look of sheer contempt, she said nothing more.

"There are times," said Martina, watching her husband get ready for bed, "when I am simply not certain how to lead this team."

He yawned wearily. "You are the team leader, not the team pastor. You should be understanding that."

"If you didn't have such a heavy Russian accent—and by the way, it's getting heavier. When I first met you it was almost imperceptible, now it's thick. You're faking it, mister cowboy boots."

He climbed in beside her. "But you did not finish. What if my accent was not so strong?"

"Then you wouldn't be so adorable."

"This is not being the issue to stick to."

"Just say, *you're not sticking to the issue.*"

He replied with frustration, "I cannot get the idioms all to be correct. You might be giving me the break."

She sighed, and he answered with an exaggerated shrug. With her finger she traced the outline of his lips, then his ear. She wondered at the force that had aligned the constellations for her to love this man.

Then he said, "If Gretchin or anyone else is not being happy working for the Agency, she can leave the work and just go paint the trees or do the something else."

"Is that an example of Russian sympathy?"

"No," he replied, "it is not."

"I recall that you needed a little sympathy at one time."

"Yes, I did, and I was happy that you were there to listen to me. And I want to be listening to Gretchin. I do not complain about her complaining. I am only complaining if it does not stop, and I am fearing that it will not stop. For all of her being the insensitive one here, she is not the insensitive one out there, I think. She does not really want to kill people. It is especially difficult for her, even if they are very bad people."

She looked into the blue eyes. "Now you are showing not just sympathy, but empathy."

"Yes," he said, nodding vigorously, "it is true, I admit it. I was the first in the team to shoot somebody. Connors, Packard, Bobbie Lee, they are professionals, they have all killed many times. But I am not an assassin, and it was very difficult for me. I still think about it very often. I want to say that I have found the peace about it, but I am not certain that I have found the peace. Maybe it is not something I can find. I am sorry like that for Gretchin. She only wanted to paint people, not kill them. . . . But sympathy is not the end of the story, I am saying. Gretchin is like all of us, she must be able to do the work, or she must simply get out of the work."

"Of course," she said softly. "And we're all thinking exactly the same thing. . . . So, you don't think we should say anything to Gretchin?"

He shook his head. "No. We should just be walking away from it, as you say. It will take the natural course."

"All right," she breathed. "We'll do that. . . . Now, pull the covers over us, Mr. Osipov, please . . . and touch me all over, please."

CHAPTER 3

Two weeks later, Kessler arrived at the Estate for one of his visits. Amiable as always, he showed up like a coach, a sidekick agent at his heels, and sat rubbing his hands together with enthusiasm.

"But still no computers, Paul?" queried Martina at length.

"Sorry," he answered, "but I'm afraid, no. For anything else, yes. For shopping, yes, sure that would be all right. But for this work, in any form, absolutely *no*."

"You know," she ventured, "there are smarter phones for smarter people."

"Okay," he sighed. "I hate to press my point, but this is part of my theory. I want this team to stick to natural communication. Just use your old phones. The new technology, smart phones, computers, the internet, is a distraction, not an aid, to natural communication. Even the professionals here are not Googling their way through this work. I've asked them not to. Leonard said he wouldn't waste his time, anyway. ... My theory, as you know, rests upon natural communication and strategy. You can argue, you can fight, whatever you want to do, to get the project completed, but please, no distracting technology." He glanced around at them. "Everybody still all right with that?"

"Oh sure," said Maggie, "if the slider on Martina's phone pops again, we'll get her one of those new flip phones."

When the general chuckling receded, he continued, "And again, no GPS. Use maps, draw them, call each other on the phone, text if you want, argue over it, swear because of it, but no GPS."

"And if we get lost?" asked Martina.

"I'll take the chance. No GPS."

Bradley, who had been eyeing Connors' sweater, imagining the gun hanging there in the flash bra, looked up suddenly. "So, Bobbie Lee, another pie?"

"No," was the drawled answer. "Carrot cake t'night. Both the cake and the frostin' are my own recipe."

Then Kessler asked Gretchin, without using her name, "How are you?"

For a moment she looked at him, wondering how it was that nature provided such people to dominate the earth. She wanted to tell him to kiss her ass, but as the thought of his lips on her skin turned her stomach, she said simply, "I'm okay, thanks."

He smiled, then said, "I have to say, you did a marvelous job, Gretchin. I was—"

"Amazed?" she offered.

"No, I was going to say *proud*, but maybe that's not the word I should use."

"It's corny."

He folded his arms. "Yes, well, maybe there isn't a good word, but your work was professional."

Frowning at this, Bradley queried, "But don't you think there might have been a cleaner way to do it, Paul?"

Kessler cocked his head. "What do you mean?"

A grin. "I don't know, I just thought, well, there was blood all over the place, it was a really gory scene. When she got in my car I had to ask her not to touch anything. She had blood and flesh all over her, even on her face."

Stiffening, her face reddening, Gretchin said, "Shut up, Bradley."

"Why should I?" he returned, his eyes large. "Know how much that car cost? And you simply *got in*, stuff all over you, like you just stepped out of a slaughterhouse. That's leather, Gretchin, leather. Know what the whole interior smells like now? It stinks, that's what."

Her eyes narrowed. "Oh, now we have it, don't we? I do the job, I'm standing in the road, waiting for you to finally show up in your sports car, and you're concerned that I might mess up your *interior*?"

He thrust both hands forward. "Money, Gretchin. It costs money to clean it. It stinks."

"I shot him, Bradley. I killed the man in his own car, and you have a problem with me getting into yours?"

He shrugged. "It's money, that's all I'm saying."

"Yeah," she said, fire in her voice, "but what's really bothering you, Bradley?" Here she pointed to herself. "I shot him, and you didn't. You got to drive me home, that's all. Made you look like some high school kid talking about his car's fucking horsepower, didn't it? Made you look like a real pussy, didn't it?"

He folded his arms. "No, it didn't. I'm just saying, *I* wouldn't have made such a mess, that's all."

"No, you're jealous."

He stuck his chin out at her. "I am not. I'm thinking about efficiency. There's nothing wrong with that. Prove there is, Gretchin, go ahead, prove there is."

"You were jealous," she taunted, pointing her finger at him. "And now you really look like a pussy, you're concerned about your car's interior."

"You're a liar!" he shouted. "You can't even shoot a man. What, afraid you'd miss?"

Now she got up, took a step toward him, and pointed down at him. "I didn't miss, fucker, and I haven't missed you. I've nailed you, haven't I?"

Instantly Kessler was beside her. "Please, Gretchin, sit down, you've made your point. Please, please, here."

When they were both seated again, Bradley smirked at her, and she took the gum from her mouth and threw it at him. But he took it up and threw it back at her, yelling at her to stop it.

"You're a goddamn asshole, Bradley," she fired back, "and you know it."

"Please, you two," put in Martina. "We have other business here today, if you don't mind."

Kessler, regaining his composure, rolled his eyes in relief. "Thank you, Martina. Yes, please, let's just all calm down." Glancing at the agent for support, he found only the bulging eyes and distinct expression of someone who had found the scene particularly entertaining.

Maggie then said, "Paul, why don't you tell us what you came to tell us."

"What?" he muttered. "Yes, yes, that's right, that's good, I will." Then, brightening, he said, "Well, I have a new project to announce, but I did want to ask about . . . well, about how you're all doing, how you're holding up."

Gretchin eyed him. "You mean, psychologically?"

"Uh, well, yes, Gretchin."

"Which of course means, how we're holding up psychologically, knowing that we have become instruments of destruction in your hands?"

He flushed, then grinned. "Blunt!" he blurted, with a wincing chuckle. "You're always so blunt, Gretchin. Please. Try looking at life from a more positive perspective. . . . I am simply asking how you *all* are holding up emotionally under the weight of service that you've given." He looked around at them. "Osipov, how are you doing? You were the first under fire, so to speak."

Gretchin scratched her tattoo. "I wouldn't say *under*."

"Yes," he replied with a chuckle. "Yes, you're right, Gretchin, yes. The lady was the one under fire. Very good."

Stanley winced. "I would not say *lady*."

Kessler's eyes grew. "And you're right, too. Yes, yes, that's correct. She was not a lady. Very good, excellent, Mr. Osipov. ... But, how are you holding up?"

The Russian became solemn. "I am not doing well, I think."

"You have a way, Stanley, of maybe leaving things half said. Could you elaborate?"

"I do not have a complaint, I am only saying that I am changed inside."

"Yes? How so, would you say?"

"I do not feel more complete."

Kessler blinked, cast another glance at the sidekick, then looked intently at Stanley. "That's a little abstract. Can you live with it or not?"

"When I weigh the positives and negatives, the answer is yes, but I cannot exactly go skipping along from one project to the next oblivious that I have taken a life. It is a weight. I understand that the weight of allowing a criminal to take the lives of more victims would be worse, but it does not completely make me feel like a better person." And looking at Martina, he asked, "Is that good wording?"

"Yes," she replied softly, looking into his blue eyes. She wanted to say more, but knew she couldn't. What she could not say was that she felt somehow thankful for his sensitivity, his tenderness. It might have gone the other way, nature might have bestowed upon her someone else, someone cruel and eager to kill, or even someone worse, a coward. But here was a man brave and true and yet tender.

Kessler, thoughtful for a moment as he too looked into the Russian's eyes, finally queried, "Do you think you're experiencing remorse?"

"Well," said Stanley, glancing toward the ceiling, "I will be telling you. The answer is yes. Not for stopping the criminal, but maybe, for being part of the human race."

"Sure, sure," was the reply. "I understand. I don't like being part of the human race, either, sometimes. That's what responsibility's all about. Sometimes, you just have to live with the weight you're given to carry. I'm sure we all understand that." As the Russian's eyes seemed to betray a wish to end the exchange, Kessler continued. "So. Is everyone else okay? Anything else to share?"

"*Share?*" repeated Gretchin, incredulous, her eyes going shut. "What are you now, our goddamn pastor? I've got a gun in my purse that I used to take the life of another human being, and you ask if I have something to share? What's to share, for God's sake? I know I killed him, you know I killed him, everyone in this room knows, thanks to Bradley here, that I practically blew his fucking head off. So, what's to share, pastor Paul? Maybe now you want us all to pass out hymnbooks and sing."

"Now, Gretchin," he said, extending his hand benevolently, as if to calm her, "don't go over the top. It's a good word, *share*. Sharing is good. There's nothing wrong with asking it that way. Let's not get excited."

"I'm not excited," she returned calmly, "I'm just telling you that I agree with Stanley. This is not the kind of work you do and just have a pizza afterward."

Startled, he stared at her for a moment, then nearly crooned, "I understand that, Gretchin, I really do. Don't think I'm cold, I'm not, trust me. And listen, everybody, I know it's difficult to do what you do, and that's precisely why I asked the question. A lot of people can't continue in the work and simply have to leave, either take to a desk, resign, or even retire, and you know all that, I'm sure. So, thanks, Gretchin and Stanley, for being straightforward about it. . . . Personally, I think you both are doing quite well, considering your backgrounds, and I commend you. But of course, you're the ones, all of you, who have to decide whether you want to continue or not."

Packard, who had crumpled himself around a cup of coffee, as though to hoard it, occasionally showed his disgust at the whole discussion by grunting, slishing up the coffee, and then smacking his lips with satisfaction. Connors, quiet as an altar mouse, exhibited her disdain via an expression that declared she was enduring utter nonsense. Bobbie Lee, reaching repeatedly for more cookies, merely grinned, as though watching comedy theater.

Observing them, Kessler cleared his throat, and added, "At least, it is difficult for most of you, those of you who are not used to this kind of work. For our professionals, now, it's not so difficult. But yes, for most of us, it can be a burden. I empathize. I've had to do this kind of work myself, at least for a time. I was a field agent, and it was difficult, I can assure you."

Bobbie Lee then jovially offered, "It's pritty hard when the funding drops, I can tell you that. But I think, as long as the money's there and the support, well, shit and hell's bells, let's rock and roll. But when I start havin' to buy my own goddamn ammunition, you're gonna hear about it, so let's not go there."

He blinked, then nearly spoke, but closed his mouth. "Yes," he replied at length, "the funding is important, yes, thank you, Bobbie. You know, speaking of funding, how is everyone with that? Is everyone being paid regularly, no glitches?"

Gretchin replied softly, "But we weren't speaking of funding."

"No," he returned immediately, his tone apologetic. "No, I understand that, Gretchin. ... Let me just say this one final thing. If it's any consolation, this team has done some marvelous things to help society. In the Texas project, you stopped the development of a drug empire, and that's no exaggeration." He held his hands out before them, as if making an appeal.

She was quick to respond. "No we didn't, we just made room for the next one."

"But—"

"No, really," she continued, "these people are just standing around waiting to take each other's place. That's what happens when you tell people they can't do something. It makes them want to do it more, because forbidding it makes it exciting, exotic. Taking illegal drugs is like having forbidden sex. When we pass these laws, we virtually create the drug empires."

He slumped wearily against the couch cushions, his face filled with futility. He stared at her, closed his mouth again, and turned to Martina, as if to plead for help.

"We know what you're saying, Paul," Martina responded. "We appreciate what you're saying. But Gretchin has a point. It's good to know we can help society by stopping the criminal who is victimizing it, but nothing's that simple. The whole syndrome of crime and justice is cyclic, not linear, and Gretchin's right, the Mexicans are standing in line to sell their drugs to the Chinese or the Americans or whoever isn't supposed to have them and now wants them."

"Well," he said, "I simply want you folks to know that you're doing a lot of good."

She smiled. "I would rather side with society than with the criminal, but again, nothing's that simple."

Momentarily he said, "Well, then, good, I agree." And then he offered to her and to all of them a most happy smile.

You're good at this, she thought as she watched his felicitous face. You're good at praising people, manipulating them, owning them. But you will not own us. We will be driven by our ideas, our principles, not yours. And for some reason, she suddenly felt sad. Then she found Maggie's eyes. Life is so very much easier to live through, she thought, when you have someone near you whose thinking and sympathies are like your own.

CHAPTER 4

"Well, then," he continued, apparently satisfied, "I should lay out for everyone the new project." From an inside coat pocket he extracted a small photograph and handed it to Martina. "Everybody take a look. This guy's very powerful, I should say for starters. Very powerful and very dangerous, a malignant entity."

Passing the photo to Stanley, Martina said simply, "It looks like he eats well."

A nod. "He does, yes. Corpulent. But as you can see, his appearance is fairly bland. He pretty much melds with the crowd everywhere he goes, because he simply looks like nobody. He's worth about fifty million, which isn't much on the world scale, but it enables him to follow his passion. His thing is talking to people, with money in his hand, of course."

"I do this myself," said the Russian facetiously, passing the photo to Maggie.

Ignoring the remark, Kessler continued, "His name is José Cole. He travels a lot and presents people with considerable sums of money. They in turn commit acts of sabotage, theft, piracy, murder, whatever he wants them to do."

Maggie chuckled. "So, he's got a bigger thing than just talking to people and making criminal deals."

His eyes glittered. "Oh, yes, I'm afraid he does. Put simply, he hates the western world, the whole of western humanity. He hates you, he hates me, he hates everyone you can think of and everyone you cannot think of, as long as they are part of western humanity."

"Sounds disturbed," said Bradley, chuckling and then grinning. "Who would hate me? Don't answer that, Gretchin."

Sweetly, she returned, "Who ever said I hated you, Bradley? In order to hate someone, you have to think about them, even just a little."

Kessler sighed wearily, as if from fear the two would go at it again. "Cole's disturbed, sure. He's pathological to the point of mayhem. Needless to say, there are many corpses in his wake."

Maggie grimaced. "Do said corpses smell?"

"No, they do not. They mount up and they rot, but they do not smell. This guy covers his tracks efficiently. He's very intelligent and totally screwed up. Great combination, right? He's on nobody's radar, except ours. His latest gripe against the western world is art. Apparently, he blames art museums for depriving the rest of the world of truth, beauty, or whatever, by hording art, stockpiling it."

"I am sure it does not end there," said Stanley thickly, resting one boot on the other. "He would have a lot of people on his side. This is exactly what Capitalists have done, they have bought up most of the art treasures and controlled their value. Or when the museums have art donated to them, they then charge admission in the daytime and lock everything up at night. The rich and powerful do hoard art, it is as simple as that, and then sell it back to the public in glimpses."

Kessler, his mouth open, stared at him. Then he said, "Please focus, Mr. Osipov. Remember, you're supposed to be working for *us*."

"This is true, this is true, yes."

With a shake of his head, Kessler continued, "José Cole is a pathologically angry man. He is negotiating for the destruction, or at least partial destruction, of the Philadelphia Museum of Art and possibly the MOMA in New York. And that's just for starters. We've gotten some really weird tips about his scheme, and intel has stamped everything."

Martina smiled. "And you don't want him arrested."

The reply was firm. "No. It's a go, I'm afraid. He's crazy, that's all there is to it, and he's crossed the line too many times. He has money and he's a patho case. He can't be left to the justice of society, which, as we all know, often means the mercy of society. No prison for this guy, I'm afraid. He would simply hire parole-bound inmates to work havoc when they got out, leaving himself with the perfect alibi of being in prison. This is a genuine enemy of western society. He plans and funds mayhem on a significant scale, but he will never stick his own head above ground. And he doesn't have to, thugs come pretty cheap when you've got fifty mil to throw around."

Bradley stopped twiddling his thumbs. "So, you know where he is?"

Kessler, who had been watching the thumbs, answered, "Yes, we do. He disappeared for a couple of years, and we thought he was gone. But he was spotted about a month ago in Philadelphia, in the Manayunk section actually. Surveillance tells us he lives alone and spends his evenings watching TV, of all things."

"Well," quipped Maggie, "he should stay away from the news. If you're crazy, watching the news will make you crazier."

"At least angry," added Martina.

"They are just playing you," said Stanley. "All Capitalists do this."

Kessler closed his eyes impatiently, then said, "People, please, focus here, okay? Cole, okay?"

"Sure, Paul, sure," Bradley said. "And I was wondering, if this Cole's alone, why do you need a team? Just deliver the guy a pizza."

Suppressing a chill, Kessler replied, "He lives alone, but he isn't alone."

"I know that one," put in Gretchin facetiously. "Isn't that where the goat and the pig and the rat have to get across the stream and, and—." She let her voice trail off as she looked at him, her eyes full of mockery. "I mean, a riddle? First you talk to us like we're your congregation and then you give us a goddamn riddle. Seriously?"

As Kessler flushed helplessly at this, Bradley merely sniffed, then said, "Take it easy, Gretch, give him a chance. Why do you always have to be so nasty? Just cool it."

Then Kessler said, "Sorry, Gretchin, I was only going to say that—"

"Just say it," she interrupted, "don't play."

"I won't, fine, take it easy. I was only going to say that according to the intel José Cole lives alone in this house. But he has met with two guys at the city's main library, and they have visited him in his house."

Scratching her nose, Maggie asked, "Is this man dangerous, is he armed?"

"Um, yes, we believe so, yes."

"And these contacts," queried Martina, crossing her legs, "are they armed?"

He swallowed, forcing his gaze from her legs. "We believe so, yes. At least, it would make sense for them to be. They're obviously characters, if you know what I mean. But it's worse, I'm afraid."

As Gretchin stiffened, about to respond, Martina said, "Would you just spell it out, Paul? What do you want us to do?"

Tugging at his ear, "Well, we think these contacts are the actual thugs he'll use to attack the museums. But they're off the radar, you understand, and we want to keep it that way. We don't want to put up any flags. We want you to make it look like—"

"Murder?" she offered.

"That would work, yes."

The Russian asked, "Do you have photographs of the contacts?"

He reached into his coat. "Yes, we do. . . . Here." He handed the photos to Stanley, but then gave Packard, Connors, and Bobbie Lee a hard look and said to them, "We want you to get all three, no matter what the cost. Just try not to kill any of the public."

"Any advice?" asked Martina.

"No. Develop a scheme, anything you want, as usual, but do it fast. We need them gone within a week, and that may be too late. The Agency, if I can say it, is really paranoid about it. Intel believes the two guys are bombers. Cole's rented the house for a year, but we think he'll only be there for a couple more weeks or so, just to get his campaign underway. You have to move fast, because he's going to strike and then move out, or the other way around. We have to get him before he disappears again." He shook his head, then dropped his gaze. "If you miss and he disappears, he'll be on to us. And I can't tell you how bad that would be."

Martina chuckled. "I suppose we can't seduce them, then."

"I would think not," he replied grimly. "You're team is really good, you've shown that. You're very creative, that's why we're giving the assignment to this team. And one last thing. We estimate that the chance of at least one of them getting away is high. Please don't let that happen. Whatever the cost, don't let that happen. Don't underestimate them. And when you do it, don't blink."

At supper, after Kessler and his agent had gone, a certain sobriety permeated the conversation. The warning of his parting words had left them uneasy, so that even Gretchin and Bradley avoided conflict. Stanley did not touch his wife's shoulder as he liked to do at dinnertime, and she did not seek Maggie's eyes. Bobbie Lee presented no levity with her dessert. Connors and Packard seemed to recede even further into the darkness of their worlds.

At length, Stanley pushed himself away from the table, stretched his legs out, and said, "We should be doing the plan making now. We need reasonable idea, please. We must allow for everything that might be wrong. I am not feeling good about this project."

Gretchin, her brow furrowed, replied cynically that she had actually never felt good about any of the projects. Connors stabbed at her pie. Packard smacked his lips and slurped at his coffee, but said nothing.

"Yes," Martina returned with a sigh, "we should draw out a plan right now." Touching Stanley's arm, she queried, "Any thoughts?"

"Thoughts?"

"Yes, thoughts," she returned. "You know, ideas."

"You are annoyed. You are showing it, it is in your tone."

"I suppose I am."

"At me?"

"No. At the Agency for handing us this."

"But it must be done."

She pushed her hair back. "I understand that, okay, husband?"

"So, live with it, wife. Be getting over it, as they say."

She sighed. "All right, listen," here she addressed everyone, "unless we get lucky, everything could go wrong. So, I want ideas, all ideas. As usual, we're going to think, which probably won't be enough. If we get lucky, great, we'll take that. Therefore," and pointing to him, "I want everything we can come up with. I want all the KGB stuff you can come up with."

"I was not KGB," he muttered, "I was photographer, that is all."

"Don't hide, Stanley, please. We need you to pull out everything you can from your little black murder book." And when he gave her a pained look, she said, "I know, you just took pictures, sure. But you were with them. Anything from your *experience* would be appreciated, all right?"

Avoiding her eyes, he looked at the toes of his boots. "I do not think a ploy to get inside the house will work, because this man is too paranoid, I think. You would never get in, which is meaning he would slam the door, or shoot you first and slam the door, and then there would be a standoff and he might get away, everybody might get away."

Bradley set his cup down. "We have to do it when they're all together. Otherwise, we'll be chasing the contacts, and that could get weird."

The Russian gave him a nod. "I am totally agreeing. It is Cole who has to get them there. We have to be watching for him to do it."

"But," said Maggie, "there's no time to wait for that. What if he's already made all the arrangements and doesn't need to see the contacts anymore?"

"Then," he returned, "we are lost, I think. The contacts will probably be getting away, or maybe one of them will, and the project will fail." He shrugged. "We should all wait in our cars in his neighborhood, I am thinking. If he goes out, we can follow him and be hoping to get them together, which is pathetic chance, I think. But if the contacts come to his house, we can decide how to do it there then, either shoot them in the doorway or force our way in later." And with a grin, "It does not look good, with three of them, one of them has good chance of getting away. There are too many factors in this project, I think."

Gretchin asked, "So, if he comes out of his house and gets into their car, or something like that, we should follow, right?"

He shrugged again. "Not necessarily. We should try to kill them all there in the car, I think. Maybe block the car first, you know, and all of us at once shoot them in the car, quickly."

Uneasy, she ran her fingers through her hair, then lifted her cup, and sipped.

"But," he continued, "if we have to follow them, then it would have to be on the street somewhere. I mean, if they stop and then walk. But at a stoplight we could do it, especially if their car is blocked. But there might be two cars. We cannot shoot them at the library, where he said they were meeting, or at a restaurant."

Connors grimaced. "Why not?"

Ignoring this comment, Martina said, "If they go out, I think we should follow them and get them on the street, anywhere on the street, but on the street. If we get lucky and they come to the house and go inside, we'll blow our way inside, front and back, covering for a window escape. What's everybody think? Speak up, I think we're all uneasy about this. Three of them, only one of them lives in the house, and we don't know where the others live. Something has to go wrong. I hate to be cynical, but this is the weirdest deal. And there's the time element too."

Stanley put his hands behind his head and looked toward the ceiling. "It is all right. A pep talk is not required."

"Good," she said. "I don't give them, and you people don't need them. Actually, for this project, I think I need one. But we're going to get these guys."

"So, now you are positive. I am loving it. Who goes in?"

She looked at each of them. "Bradley, Gretchin, why don't you cover the back this time. Don't go in, though. Stay on the phone, and we'll call you if we want you to go in. Then of course, just Bradley, with Gretchin on the windows." And looking at Connors, who merely sipped at her tea, she said, "Kelly, I think you and Len and Stanley should go in the front. Maybe you first."

With her eyes still upon Connors, who made no response but seemed interested only in her tea, Martina stole a moment to marvel at the woman. There was something irresistible, even magical about her. It did not seem to come from her astounding looks, glamorous as they were, but from deeper, much deeper inside her, where in everyone the light and the darkness struggle. She seemed so like the old Samurai, yet without a normal sense of honor. In fact, everything about her seemed to do with another world, perhaps an angelic one. In any case, there was something ethereal about this knight of death, something that both attracted you and repelled you, something that instinctively made you careful.

Then Stanley put in, "I am having a second thought," he said heavily. "I am not happy."

"You are from Russia, for God's sake," she replied, "you are not expected to be happy."

"But happy or not, the second thoughts are still there," he said, the sides of his mouth turned down.

A long, impatient blink. "Meaning?"

He was deliberate. "I am thinking that we should not blast our way in. That is too much the slow way, and somebody will get killed, I am certain of this. We should knock on the door carefully, with some pretense, and then make the quick attempt there."

Rolling her eyes, "A pretense? You're the one who said a ploy wouldn't work."

A shrug. "I changed my mind."

Perturbed, she turned to Connors. "So, Kelly?"

Connors looked up at her. "The pretanse is good, t'at'll work," she said, "et always seems to work. The problem is, somebody es likely to gat away. I agree et looks bad, pretty fuckin' bad. There's too many variables. Ef et's joost at the house, we can't pull out our weapons on the front parch and fill the whole place weth shet, they moight gat out the back. Blastin' t'rough a door, even a loight door, can take toime, and by then they're out the fuckin' back or we've got a standoff."

"So, make us a proposal."

"I'm not proposin' nothin'. I'm joost sayin' we moight have to gat the door, or doors, open, pariod. And the whole t'ing's gotta be done loightnin' queck."

"Correct," rasped Packard. "And he'll never open the door. He'll answer it, but he'll never open it, except for his own guys. If he's close to making a strike, he'll be wary."

"So," said Martina, "a proposal, Len?"

"No. I'm not big on plans, just guns. But I will take my shotgun, I think."

"Kelly," she said, "no proposal? Sure?"

"I'm not big on 'am, either."

"Nothing from your past could help us?"

Eyes sparkling, "What past es that, gletterin' swords 'n carpses?" And when there was no response, "I've already said, expariance tells me not to make too many plans. T'ink about et, but don't plan for much."

The silence that followed this was palpable. No one had forgotten their first encounter with Kelly Connors as the cold woman in the gray suit who escorted them to the meeting with Kessler at the hotel, where the first project was unfolded, or his introduction of her as 'just doing the coffee.' They had since seen her practically eat flesh with a gun and had come to appreciated the sheer lethality of the woman. All of them believed she had been IRA.

Turning her gaze, Martina queried, "Bobbie Lee, anything?"

"None," was the answer. "I agree with Killy 'n Lin. Plan a little, maybe, but not much. Clean yer guns, be creative, and rock 'n roll."

But Bradley said to Connors, "Nobody's implying anything about the IRA, Kelly, but how would they have handled something like this? We need your expertise, wherever it came from, just like we need Osipov's."

She gave a quick sniff and then said to him, looking directly at him, "Fuck you."

He cleared his throat. "Sorry."

But then she puffed her cheeks out and blew air toward the ceiling. As if reluctantly, she said to them all, "We would've gunned 'am down at the door—foive mellimeters, full auto—or joost blown tham up. But Kassler doesn't want us usin' stuff or even real automatics."

Maggie groaned. "Well, I'm glad he doesn't. Keep it simple, please. I don't know the first thing about explosives and don't want to, thank you very much. And if I can barely use a .38, what in heaven's name would I do with a machine gun?"

"Prob'ly nothin'," quipped Connors. "But two or t'ree of 'am full auto should do the treck. Roight at the door, whole fuckin' front of the house, turn et to shet. Drop 'am loike shet, I can promise yous."

Maggie smiled amicably. She had witnessed the woman's kill skills often enough to believe everything about her and anything she said. Such a beautiful woman, to be sure, with a body that, if it weren't for its scars from bullet holes, any glamour photographer in the world would love to bring into focus.

"No need to promise, Kelly," she replied, "I'll take your description as accurate."

Connors put her cup down. "Look, yous, there's not much point to guessin'. Et never works. Joost wait till we gat there. We'll play et by ear."

Bradley, who had been staring at Connors' hair, her face, suddenly became aware of Gretchin's watchful eye. Clearing his throat a little, he looked down at his plate and then shifted the position of his water glass.

The Russian shrugged, raising his eyebrows. "It is not much of a plan," he said. "KGB never used plan, either, and they killed just about everybody."

Martina looked at him for a moment, then said to everybody, "Well, I guess that's it then. It looks like we're going to be doing a lot of car sitting, waiting for them to show up. It's ridiculous, the whole thing, but there's no time to work out strategies for different scenarios. . . . Okay, Kelly, we'll do it that way. We'll drive to Philly tomorrow. Everyone goes, except Maggie, I think. Don't think we'll need you on this one, Maggie, but we might need Bobbie Lee's fire power."

"Oh, that's fine with me, dear," said Maggie, reaching for her tea. "I don't mind staying home. The dogs and I will watch over things here. Just be careful, everyone, please."

The Estate's two residential structures formed an L and were connected by an enclosed walkway. Both houses, double-storied, with airy attics and cool, dry cellars, faced a driveway that encircled a stone fountain. Maggie said the fountain was a bird bath, since it did not work and only collected rainwater. On the first floor of the larger house, which Stanley dubbed the Big House, were located the living room, dining room, and kitchen. The first floor of the smaller house, which Bradley named the Den, provided two recreation rooms, a tiny library, and a spacious reading room. Martina and Stanley, Maggie, Gretchin, and Connors had taken second-floor bedrooms for themselves at the Big House, while Bradley, Packard, and Bobbie Lee had chosen bedrooms on the second floor of the Den.

Just before bed, returning from the shower, Bobbie Lee stopped Packard in the hall. "Greasin' the guns?" she queried. It was a joke gun people always kept at hand.

"Hell no," he replied with theatrical gruffness. "Grease your own guns, lady."

"What's the matter," she teased, "afraid they'll blow up? An old grime like you shouldn't mind losin' a few fingers."

She eyed appreciatively the naked jackass rig. The double-holster harness, well known among detectives, always seemed to exude a certain glamour. Although she had at one time toyed with wearing one herself, she knew the famous leather setup had its negatives and was even held in notoriety by some for dangling its guns instead of holding them fixed. It was not unknown that a sloppy pull could get you killed. Still, she considered, worn by the likes of Packard, a killer's killer, the slung rig, especially when filled with heavy Smiths, was impressive to the point of being inspirational.

"You're funny, lady," he threw back with a grin. "I don't need fingers missing. I'll stick to light oil, thanks. Go grease your own guns. Fill 'em with grease, stick 'em in the dirt, and pull the trigger, for all I care."

From the first, he had liked her, this sassy bitch, as he called her, from Tennessee. It was no secret that he admired her. She could have been his daughter, for her age and spunk. He liked women with muscles and courage, and she had both.

She sighed, leaning agaist the wall in her robe. "So, what do you think 'bout tomorra?"

He bit his lower lip gently before answering. "Don't know. It isn't something I'd normally walk into."

"Yeah, I do see a little doubt in your face."

"Well, I'll say this, I've never seen anybody meaner than Connors. If she goes after somebody, that somebody's going to end up in a box. You've seen her in action, too. She's tougher than spider soup. Anybody that marries that woman will never argue with her."

"No, I shouldn't think they would."

After a moment he asked, "Something bothering you?"

"I don't know," she said, "guess I'm worried about everybody's luck runnin' out. It happens. It's math."

He sniffed. "Simple arithmetic, I'd say. But, so what?"

"So, ever think of retirin'?"

A chuckle. "And do what, sit around all day and play solitaire and drink? Clean my guns on weekends just for fun? . . . I kill people. I'd miss it."

Pushing away from the wall, she gave the towel on her shoulder a tug. "Me too," she replied and then walked away.

His eyes followed her until she went into her room. He imagined her taking the robe off, slipping into bed and sleeping with the Smith & Wesson. Then he turned and walked to the bathroom.

CHAPTER 5

Manayunk, Philadelphia

It was early when Stanley parked the SUV on the narrow Manayunk street. He left the engine running and the air on. He did not look at Martina, though he longed to. She would be beautiful. But then he did look and caught her profile as she opened her phone. Behind him, Connors, who had seemed especially quiet during the trip, sat silent. Beside her, Bobbie Lee, who had complained more than once that she did not like riding in the middle, did her best to arch her back for relief.

"I'm gittin' my own vehicle," she said, "maybe a motorcycle, but I ain't sittin' in the middle anymore, I guarantee it."

"This is a huge car," he said. "You Americans complain too much. You are privileged and still you complain."

"Hey," she shot back, "you got your own seat. You try sittin' in the middle and then do your talkin', mister."

Holding up both hands, "I always used to sit there. I sat in middle of very small car, between two KGB agents, and I held camera on lap. It was tiny car. I am speaking from the experience."

"Tell you what, you can sit here on the way back, and I'll drive, how's that suit you, pal?"

He shrugged. "It does not suit me."

"Oh, Lord, listen to him. Would you like coffee and donuts too as you stritch yer legs out? That's practic'ly a lounge chair, mine isn't, bubba. I can tell you this, I'm gittin' my own vehicle, that's for sure."

Martina muttered, as if to herself, "I'm glad Maggie stayed back. I don't know why."

Packard merely grunted at this and gave his coat pocket a feel for the speedloaders. Pulling one of the magnums from its nest and then replacing it, he recalled reading as a child how Doc Holliday had regularly spent hours practicing drawing his gun. Amazing, he thought, what things stayed with you. Here he was in his sixties, bullet scarred and mean, and still he would sit in the back seat of a car and remember a kid's impressions. Stupid. Life was just that—so goddamn stupid.

Connors, still silent, ran her fingers around the brim of her cap, but did not put it on. She was to impersonate a representative from the city gas company. Surreptitiously she felt the revolver's bulge as it hung between her breasts in the flash holster. As she would have to yank her official shirt up to get at it, she tugged until the last button just cleared her belt. "No snags," she muttered almost imperceptibly, "no fuckin' snags."

When Martina's phone buzzed, she looked at its screen and announced, "It's Gretchin. They're in the alley behind the house. They're ready."

Stanley, watching two men who had come around the corner of the block and were walking toward the house, said suddenly, "Our people? Is it actually to be our people? This is too easy, I am thinking. Have we just won at roulette?"

"Not quite," replied Packard, his eyes glinting as he watched the men.

Connors, her eyes trained on them as they approached, said, "Mother of God, et's tham. We've got about tan saconds, I'd say." And then she said, her voice steady as frozen steel, "We've gotta go now. Let me go alone, I'll do et, et's gotta be now." And even as the men turned and began to climb the front steps to the porch of the house she took up the clipboard and yellow flashlight and opened her door.

Packard drew one of the magnums. His eyes followed her as she crossed the narrow street and began to climb the steps to the porch where the men had rung the bell. He did not doubt her prowess, her ability to kill three men with the five shots from her flash-bra gun and if necessary the five from her backup under the back of her shirt. Doubting Kelly Connors with a gun approaching three men was like doubting Einstein with chalk approaching a blackboard. Somehow you just didn't question the outcome. No, he did not doubt her or that her two guns and ten shots would be enough. But Nature, or luck, or fate, or whatever you called it, had a perverse way of saying *no* just when you needed a *yes,* and in that case, of course, a thousand shots wouldn't be enough.

Stanley dropped the windows an inch for listening, hooked a finger in the latch, ready to push his door open, and held his breath as Connors finished climbing the steps. "One glitch," he whispered, "and we go."

Just as the two men turned to her another man pulled the house door inward and then pushed the storm door open. Although he had not stuck his face out, she recognized him as the target and announced with authority, "Gas Comp'ny. There's a break around the carner, and et's sarious. Nobody should smoke."

Hesitating for just a second, the man pushed the door open wider and said, "I haven't smelled a thing. No leak here."

"Take a look at this," she replied, holding the clipboard out for him to take.

As his hand closed upon the clipboard she let the flashlight fall, yanked up her shirt, ripped the revolver down, stuck it in his face and fired twice—*Pop! Pop!* Even as he dropped she spun right and shot the man nearest the step, also in the face, for he was very close, and as he collapsed, not waiting for him to hit the boards, instantly turned and fired twice into the third man's chest. As this third man fell backward against the house and began to collapse she deftly returned the gun to the bra holster, pulled her rear shirt tail out, and produced the backup .38. He now clutched his chest miserably and gave her a horrific stare of hatred. Instantly she put the gun's muzzle to his forehead, even as he sank lower down the wall, and fired.

Then she pulled open the storm door, which had sprung shut, stepped inside, and shot the man, now a corpse, twice in the head. Quickly stepping out again, she precisely shot both fallen men once again in the head. Then, with eerie calmness, she returned the backup to its holster, picked up the flashlight and clipboard, descended the steps, unhurriedly crossed the street, and pulled the SUV's door open.

"I figured," said Bobbie Lee as Connors got in, "you didn't need me to open the door for you." And then, "Jesus, that was fast! That was about the fastist thing I ever saw in my life. That was like you were dancin' or somethin'. Shit! I'll bet that's a mess on that porch."

Closing the windows, Stanley, suddenly aware that his mouth was still open, closed it. Then he pulled the shift down and carefully moved the SUV from the curb.

As he did so, Martina spoke into her phone, "It's done, Gretchin. Drive." At the end of the block she said, "Look at all these houses. Where is everybody?"

"Asleep, maybe," muttered Stanley, "but I think they will be awake now, thanks to us. They will just call the police and then walk their dogs."

"It's a pretty street, quaint."

"It is," chimed Bobbie Lee, "but I prefer livin' in the country."

Less than a minute later Martina's phone vibrated. After reading the text, she said, "Good. She says they're out and on the street. Let's go home."

It was not until they were on the expressway, heading west, that anyone spoke again. As Martina looked back at Connors, who sat placidly looking out her window toward where the rocky ledges met the roadway, she considered again this terrible woman. It was a becoming profile, suited to such beauty. The face, despite the specks of blood, could have been that of a cherub, and in fact, no one would believe that it belonged to someone who had just brutally shot three men to death. But life was like that, she thought, recalling the gory scene on the porch. You could think one thing and even see one thing, while reality was actually quite another thing. Here was this killer of killers, gazing serenely out her window as would an innocent child. As Martina turned forward to look out the windshield it was Connors who spoke.

"Holy Mary," she muttered, running a hand down her front, "I've ruined me fuckin' shairt."

Martina looked back again at the beautiful face, the radiant hair, the sumptuous mouth, but then also at the bits of flesh and spots of blood on the shirt. "Yes," she replied, "it's on your face too, I'm afraid."

"But it was good work," Packard said, his eyes fixed upon the Schuylkill River. And then he added, "I guess, lady, you didn't need a magnum today."

Connors chuckled to herself at the compliment, then said, "Guess I dedn't. .38's are faster, much faster."

With a nod, "Grantcha that.".

The Russian, who had been checking his mirror, said, "They are behind us now." And as

Martina looked out the back he added, "He must get rid of that car. It is too bright, I am thinking."

She squinted. "Are they arguing?"

"Yes," he replied, glancing again at the mirror. "When are they not arguing?"

She looked at him. She loved the things he said. Everything about him, she seemed to love, to adore. At times she felt ashamed of her devotion to him. The very tone of his voice seemed often, for her, to take precedence over the wisdom of his words. It was not, of course, that he was not wise, for he was, and knowledgeable too; it was just that, when the marbles of the inner human being were traded, which is to say, when it came to the core realities of heart and soul, she loved him beyond reason.

Lancaster County

Later, in bed, she touched him and said softly, "Rub my back. I will pay you."

He slid a leg across the backs of her legs, pushed her nightgown up, and pressed himself against her body. Tenderly he began to massage the tight muscles of her back. "Rubles or dollars?" he whispered. "How will you pay me?"

She gave a short laugh. "And you're a Communist? Really? You should be ashamed of yourself."

"I am ashamed, yes. Just as you said it I was beginning to experience deep shame." He kissed her arm and continuing to massage the muscles running beside her spine.

"Well, you should be. And what would you buy with the rubles? Property? It's all disgusting, and what would you do with property when you got it, look for peasants to suffer at tillage while you lay around stroking your wife?"

He moved his fingers up to her neck. "You are not relaxing. The muscles are just as tight. Take a deep breath and relax."

She obeyed, then said, "I will not pay you in money. I will pay you in potatoes, one potato at a time. This will keep you pure and free from the corruption of going into business, becoming rich, buying property, and lording it over me."

"Where is this potato I am being promised?"

"Between my legs," she replied.

"Good," he said. "I would like to see this potato. I will look for it now."

"Do that, please."

Late in the afternoon of the next day, Kessler placed a freshly brewed cup of coffee at the center of his desk and sat down. He should have had kids, for then, like other dads, he would have an after-school game to attend. He enjoyed it when colleagues talked about their kids. Carefully he moved the cup perpendicularly away from him and reached for his phone.

"Hi, Martina. Listen, I'm satisfied with every-thing, so just consider the project as completed. Good job. Got a new project, so I'll come out in a couple of days and lay it out."

"Not going to let the weary rest, huh?"

"Right," he said with a chuckle, reaching for the cup. "So, just tell everybody to relax, then, okay?"

"Sure."

He sipped at the coffee, then said, "Actually we'll only need two of you on this one, Kelly and Bobbie. So, you can let them know at least that and tell the others to rest."

"I will."

He winced at her cold reply. He did not like cold replies. In fact, he hated them. Why in God's name should she answer him that way? "What's the matter, Martina," he said momentarily, "need a vacation?"

"Might be nice."

Bitch, he muttered to himself, placing the cup on the blotter. "I think that can be arranged," he said. "Need a little swim time, huh? That's reasonable. You've all done a great job."

Again coldly, "Thanks."

Supressing his anger, he said, "Talk to you later. I'll call."

He turned the phone off, put it down, and picked up the cup. Perhaps it was time to start speeding things up. It couldn't go on forever. What, should he let them retire? The pricks had overstayed, that's all. Out with the old, let's go. His theory had been proven, it was time, let's go, get it done. It only made sense that they, all of them, the whole team, should now be ushered from the stage, actually from the theater. Shoot them? No, of course not. But he could turn the dial up, way up. How had these people survived so long?

CHAPTER 6

The patio behind the Big House was spacious and cool and had become one of the favorite places to relax for every member of the team. Although Maggie had complained that the two oaks at its corners made a daily sweep-up practically necessary, she acknowledged the beneficial shade they provided. As no one else had seemed interested in helping with such maintenance, at least to her satisfaction, she came to accept the task and had even bought herself a special broom. Now, as Kessler, his driver, and the team sat on patio chairs and sipped tea, she scowled at a twig she had missed.

"I have a new project," Kessler said at length, brushing away a gnat. "It's lovely out here, isn't it?" As no one responded to this, except the agent, who only gave a quick nod, he continued, "Yes, well, I have a new project. But we'll only need Kelly and Bobbie on this one. Everybody else can relax or actually just take a vacation, if you want. What do you think?" He looked around at them and then queried enthusiastically, "Gretchin, how about you, a vacation, a little time beside a nice pool somewhere?"

Giving him a squint, as if to express the hopelessness of trying to communicate with someone imbecilic, she drew a leg up and then answered, "Why the hell not?"

"Yes, well," he said wearily, "good."

"Where can we go?"

He sipped again at his tea. "Cape May would be lovely," he answered, "except that's where Kelly and Bobbie will be." Here he grinned, as if expecting laughter. When there was none, he said, "Just find a place you like and go there."

Gretchin offered back, "I'd love to tell you where to go sometime, Paul."

He stared at her as she pushed a handful of red hair behind her ear. God, he hated impudent women. Maybe the filthy bitch could just kill herself, or something, he thought. It would save him a lot of trouble. But as he looked around at the others he realized that not one of them seemed amicable in the least. Finally he said, "Yes, well, you need a rest, Gretchin, all of you do, I'm sure. So pick a place and take about a month off. And Kelly, Bobbie, when you finish the project, just take off yourselves, okay?"

Gretchin smirked. "Is the Agency paying for it, or are we on our own?"

"Um, yes, well, the latter actually. I just mean, feel free to take the time off."

"That's so goddamn cute," she retorted. "First we put our lives on the line and then we have to pay for resting from it."

He held his hands apart, as if to ask help from heaven. "That's why we pay you a good salary, Gretchin."

"A good salary, considering what we do? That's an insult."

He looked at her helplessly. "Well, it's the government we're talking about, not Fort Knox."

"I suppose Fort Knox is in private hands."

"No, no," he returned. "Gretchin, you're coming across as, well, disgruntled. Am I correct about that?"

"No," she replied, mimicking his look of helplessness. "Sure, I'll go on vacation. And I'll pay for it. Forget it."

Martina, clearing her throat, sat forward. "Tell us about the project, Paul. Who's in Cape May?"

He sighed with weariness from the exchange. "Uh, yes, well, um, birders actually."

As he seemed to pause, she said, "Go on, please."

"Yes, well, do you believe it? Birders."

Stanley crossed his stretched-out legs. "I like the birds," he said simply. "I am somewhat of the birder, myself."

"Well, good for you, Stanley. Yep, you're a birder. Okay, great." If he hated impudent women, he loathed smart-assed Russians. Eyeing the cowboy boots, he said, "It's probably an interesting field to get into, if you like cameras, which you do, of course."

"Are you being the diplomat?"

And now only by looking away could he suppress his anger. He wanted to say that he considered him to be a dirty piece of slavic shit, but drawing his breath slowly for self-control, he said, "The bird sanctuary there, out at what is called Cape May Point, attracts birders from all over North America. Our next target frequents the place." Here he reached for his tea cup. "The woman is from Canada, you know."

"I like Canadians," Gretchin said.

"I don't care if you do, Ms. Wheeler," he shot back. "Just keep it to yourself if you must like the Canadians, is that fair enough, do you think?"

But she had rattled him and was satisfied and so replied with a mere, "Sure."

"The woman, our target," he continued, "is a vicious human being. That's the only way to describe her. She's English but lives in Montreal. We thought she worked behind a cover of being a birder, but we discovered her interest in birds is genuine. She just likes to do her dirty work stuff on the side, so to speak. Criminality is her hobby, and birding, her real interest. That's where the Agency comes in. . . . You're going to love this. She's an assassin." Retrieving his cup, he sipped and waited for their response.

"You mean," said Connors, "loike us."

"No, Kelly, I did not mean that," he replied, annoyed. "You work for the government, but she's a criminal."

"One couldn't be both, I suppose."

He shifted in his chair. "Yes, well, what we do in this business is necessary. That's why we call it service. It's not criminality, it's service."

"You can call et what you loike, but et's kellin' people, semple as t'at."

He swallowed awkwardly, "Well, that's a little blatant, I think. I like to call it service. I think that's what we should all call it, and not just call it that, but think of it like that—it's a perspective. Mr. Hopkins here would call it that, wouldn't you, Brad?"

Bradley lifted his chin. "Yes," he answered thoughtfully. "Yes, I would, and I would go further and say that it's service *to one's country.*"

"Good, see there, that's right, that's what it is, I agree. That's the way we should all be seeing it, service to our country. You folks do a great job. Nobody's complaining, at least not at the Agency. Everyone there says you're doing a really great job. You've made the world a better place, to be sure."

"You mean," put in Gretchin, her gaze upon one of the protruding butts of Packard's magnums, "we've made the world a *smaller* place."

Kessler put his hands together. "Okay, whatever. Anyway, listen, this target is a real slime ball. She has a small organization, which she formed herself, that traffics in illegal drugs. Not the recreational kind, the medical kind. Currently she markets a drug in Africa that works as a chemical abortion. Unfortunately, one in ten of the women who use it dies. Knowing this, our target has only sought to step up the traffic, like it's not only lucrative but great fun. We discovered through our sources that when she learned of the deaths she actually took steps to increase the traffic, to the tune of doubling it. A strange one, with a cauterized heart."

"Which is where we come in," said Bobbie Lee, setting a fresh batch of oatmeal cookies beside the tea tray and then taking a seat beside Connors. "Sounds like you don't like this lady very much."

His eyes brightened. "Exactly. I mean, that's exactly right, that's where you come in. If she's removed, the entire operation will cease. She's wealthy from the business and has looked into expansion to South America. I think the Pope'll come after her, if she gets down there."

With a few blinks, Bradley queried, "How do you connect all this with assassination? You said she was an assassin."

"You know, Bradley," said Gretchin, giving her hair a swipe, "sometimes you suck up just with your tone."

He reddened. "Who's sucking up? What did I do?"

"It's the way you say things."

"I have no idea what you're talking about. Don't start another argument, Gretchin, just listen to the man."

"Okay," put in Martina with exasperation. "Paul, could you continue, please. She's an assassin, right?"

A smile of relief, then, "Oh, yes, I'm afraid she is. But like I said, it's a macabre hobby, a form of distraction, I suppose, a pastime. Quite weird, I'm afraid. You would think the birding would be the hobby. The business pays for the birding, it seems, while the assassination hobby pays for itself. Very strange."

Reaching for a cookie, Maggie asked, "Who does she work for?"

"A businessman in Montreal, a low-life, himself, a snake." Then checking himself at Gretchin's chagrin, he said, "I mean, snakes are nice. I have nothing against snakes. It was just an image. . . . But um, she's worked for him twice, we know. And this is where it gets even weirder. She kills with a knife."

A frown from Maggie. "A birder who kills with a knife? Yeah, that's a funny one. Psycho?"

His eyebrows rose as he shrugged. "We don't know. And we don't care."

Then Connors said, "Sweet. Where'd she learn her shet?"

There it was again, he thought, gazing at the blond hair, the sumptuous lips, the ethereal eyes, all as if bestowed by the gods. How was it that such beauty and vulgarity ended up together? "You mean," he replied, "her assassination skills? We don't know. She had some military time. Anyway, a very nasty woman. She goes every year to Cape May, following the migrating birds. Apparently, enthusiasts go to spot the birds of prey that attack the migrating ones. It's quite the thing. September."

"Any particulars on our part?" drawled Bobbie Lee, balling up her fists and flexing the muscles in her arms the way a man would.

He watched her do this, then answered, "No. Just do it and get out. Maps of Cape May and the Cape May Point sanctuary, including footpaths of the sanctuary, are in this packet. Also three photos of the woman. She usually travels alone or with another woman, not always the same. Much of our information is sketchy. Her name is Anne Smith Strepper. She goes by *Annie*."

Connors opened the envelope and spread the photos. "Pretty as hell," she remarked. "And family?"

"None."

"You'd t'ink she could sell 'er ass. She's got some real glamour."

He looked at her bulging blouse, then replied meekly, "Yes, she does."

"A real paice o' tail. She got a man, any romance?"

He blinked slowly. "You mean, sex life? Well, that's just it. Apparently, she has no sex life. Just the business, the birds, and the little hobby. But again, our info isn't perfect."

With a chuckle, "So, what's new?"

"No need for sarcasm," he retorted softly. "Anyway, it's all yours."

"I'm t'inkin'," she said, a sparkle coming into her eyes, "we could go down as two lasbians."

As his eyes dropped from her mouth to her blouse and he imagined her going for the gun he gave his head a slight shake. Shifting his gaze to Bobbie Lee's rippling muscles, he said to Connors, "Whatever, Kelly. You know what you're doing."

She replied, "Joost fuckin' kell 'er, roight?"

"Uh, yes," he replied softly, "yes, of course. . . . That was amazing work in Philadelphia, just amazing."

As usual, there was no response from her or from any one else to his praise. But he was confident that his theory would stand. If the effect of flattery did not appear on their faces, he knew it was there in their minds. In this respect they were not different from him or anybody else. *Anybody* could be turned into a killing tool by simply subjecting him to the right negative and positive circumstances. The power of danger, success, and praise was ultimately not resistible by the human being, and these human beings were going to follow everyone else, right down the wretched tubes. He glanced around at them, wincing at their theater, their pathetic attempts to resist his praise. Finally he looked straight into Connors' eyes. He pictured her reholstering the hot .38 between her breasts.

Then he said to her, "You do know it was amazing, don't you?"

"Guess I do," she returned. "I'm the one t'at fuckin' kelled 'am."

Bradley stretched his arms. "I, personally, am more than ready for a vacation. Can't wait to find a pool somewhere. Relax, relax, relax."

With a groan, Gretchin rolled her eyes. "Yeah, and you could have one of those floating trays of beer, right there beside you in the pool, correct?"

"No, no," put in Kessler, hoping to thwart another exchange, "Bradley's right. You should all relax. That's the way I want it. You should have your vacations, you deserve the rest. And Kelly, Bobbie, you girls should take a vacation, too, when it's over. I want the best for you."

Connors looked at him as a cat would look at a mouse that it considered to be just too dirty to eat.

Bobbie Lee queried, "Is that 'cause you love us?"

"Funny," he returned with a smile. "But I do care, I really do. I want the best for you, all of you. You'll have to trust me on this."

With a chuckle, Bobbie Lee replied, "I don't think I could ever trust the government, no matter what, and that's a fact. I have a business relationship with this here government, and that's it."

"But, Bobbie," he said, "you yourself are part of the government, did you ever think of that?"

"Yeah," she replied, nodding her affirmation, "like a gun is part of an arm. The arm doesn't love the gun, and the gun doesn't love the arm. It's strictly a business relationship. It's functional, that's it. The day I believe the government loves me, I'll laugh myself to death."

"I don't know, that's pretty cynical. I believe the government does care. I couldn't live with myself otherwise."

When she did not respond further, he looked from her to Connors, then around at them all. Then, as if impulsively, he stood up and smiled. The agent, as if trained to do so, also got up and produced a smile. Martina cleared her throat, then got up.

"Thanks, Paul, for coming out," she offered. "We'll take care of it."

Merely nodding at this, he gave the agent a look of impatience. Maggie walked them to the door, then watched them from the front window. When their car had rounded the fountain, she let the curtain drop back into place.

"They're gone," she said softly as the group began to break up. "Why do I feel so cold?"

"Because," suggested Martina, tea cup still in hand, "the viable life and warmth have just driven away in a gray sedan?"

"Now, now," said her husband, "do not be picking on the poor Paul too much. People like that are necessary."

Maggie pulled her summer sweater closer around her neck. "Necessary for what?"

He shrugged, but then said, "I am not entirely certain, but every spy agency has them, so they must somehow be necessary, it is only logical. The only problem with them is when they see people like us as unnecessary."

Late in the evening Bradley put his shoes on and walked over to the Big House for a snack. In the kitchen he was glad to find Bobbie Lee just putting together a sandwich.

"Couldn't make one for me, could you?" he said, taking a seat on a bar stool.

The sandwich made, she added potato chips and set the plate on the counter. "Beer?"

"You know it. Whatcha got?"

She opened the fridge to give him a look. "Jist stocked it in. There's lager, pale ale, porter, and stout, but you wouldn't be interested in that kinda stuff, would you?"

With surprise, "Wouldn't I? Why do you say that?"

"How 'bout a Budweiser?"

"But what made you think that?"

Grabbing the bottle and then prying off its cap, she set it before him. "You git Budweiser."

"I can be sensitive," he offered defensively. "What do you think, I can't be sensitive?" And without waiting for her reply, he tipped the bottle up and chugged at it.

Gritting her teeth a little, she said, "Careful, hombre, don't git yourself drunk."

"That's an insult. Two's gonna make me drunk, right?"

She smiled to herself and then straightened a dish towel on its rack. She did not watch him eat, but busied herself with emptying the dishwasher. She did not like him. She had no time for a man this full of himself. As he bit into the sandwich she cleared the flatware from its trays and began to put the pieces away.

Gathering as many chips as he could between thumb and finger, he held them above his mouth and then dropped them in. It was convenient having her there, for he loathed making his own snacks, but he did not want to talk to her. Okay, so she could ride a motorcycle, so what? He eyed her for an instant as she bent over. He did not care for a woman with muscles. No matter how she presented herself—pants, dress, no dress—a woman with rippling arms, even a slender one like this, a woman with genuine muscles and fists was a definite turnoff. Turning back to the sandwich, he crammed in another mouthful and munched contentedly. He had not come over to see her anyway.

"You okay?" she asked, wiping her hands on the towel. "I'm goin' up."

"Sure, sure," he managed around the bread and meat. Swallowing with difficulty, he tipped up the bottle to wash the rest down. He watched her as she left.

When he had finished the sandwich, he gave the plate a tick with his finger, left the kitchen and climbed the stairs to Connors' room. Drawing his breath, he gave a double knock and waited. When the door was opened he looked at the blond hair, then into the eyes, and said, "You relax, right? I mean, you do something other than just kill people, right?"

Wearily she blinked and then replied, "Spake up."

"Want a drink?"

She watched as his eyes greedily traveled over her. Slowly she closed the door, as if to say he was not worth answering. Then she opened it again and said, "And don't be standin' outsoide me dar. Bother me again, fucker, and I'll smare your guts on the wall."

"Yeah, you and the whole IRA, I guess."

"Won't nade 'am."

He gazed into the eyes. Yes, amazingly, they were colorless, absolutely colorless. He felt his chest tighten as she met his gaze. He was not afraid of much, but yes, he was afraid of the emptiness of this woman. A man could die and go to hell in such emptiness. He wondered what had driven him to come here. A moment later, he muttered, "Okay, sure," then turned and walked away.

Back at the Den he heard a tap at his door and opened it to Packard, who stood, like the Devil himself, a bottle of Jack Daniel's in his grip.

"Can I come in?" Packard rasped through a yellow-toothed grin.

"Yeah, sure."

"Want some sour mash? Got a glass?"

Bradley nodded toward the bottle. "Bobbie Lee loves that stuff."

A pleasant chuckle. "Yep, she does. Who doesn't? I've drunk a lot of whiskey, but this is the straight shit, let me tell you. It's the pine flavor, that's what it is. I think they age it in a pine box with a corpse in it."

After rinsing out two glasses in the bathroom sink, Bradley held them out. "Not perfect, but you won't die probably."

As the gritty man poured he queried, "So, did you go see her?"

"Who?"

"Connors."

"Uh, yeah. How'd you know? What, are you snooping or something?"

"Don't have to, pal. You're pretty well stricken."

"Okay. And that's your business?"

A smile. "I guess it isn't. . . . But I did want to warn you, kind of as a friend. And I don't really have friends."

"I've noticed."

Packard threw him a look. "Yeah."

Sniffing the whiskey, "But that's all right. I've already been rejected *and* warned."

"Oh yeah? Well, I expected it. I'll tell you, I've met her kind, and I like her, don't get me wrong, but I've seen them, and they're frosted magnesium inside. You bother her too much, and she'll blow your brains out right on the sidewalk, she won't sneak about it. And she'll do it with a smile on her face, and she'll sleep like a baby at night. Again, don't get me wrong, she's nice, but she is one hell of a butcher, bud, oh yeah. She doesn't care about Kessler or the Agency or anybody really."

"You're not being a little harsh?"

"Harsh? God! I've seen her kill, pal, and so have you. There's something about it that freezes your goddamn balls, boy."

"Well, you're pretty creepy, yourself. Do you ever take those guns off, ever—what, do you sleep with that jackass rig, roll over in the night on your magnums? That's kind of nuts."

Packard drained his glass. "Actually I do sleep with my guns, but I take the rig off. I don't shower with them. Hey, but I'll bet *she* sure does. . . . I'm just warnin' you, as a friend, you mess with her too much, and the junk dealer will be crushing your Corvette up into a plastic block and they'll be sellin' your baseball card collection at the local fair. You'd be wise, as a man, I mean, to let some genuine fear run through you when you're around her, pal, I'm tellin' you, 'cause she's a real goddamn killer, more'n I am, that's for sure. She wouldn't hesitate for anything. She'd even shoot Kessler in the face just for sayin' the wrong word. She's a mean one, pal, I'm serious." He gave his head a shake. "Boy, talk about using a volcano to light your cigar. I don't want to see your corpse in her doorway, but I will see it, if you bother her, okay?"

Hanging his head, Bradley ran a hand over his crew cut, then muttered, "Yeah."

Momentarily, "You're not in love with her, are you?"

"No."

"Listen, she's not afraid of anything or anyone in the whole wretched universe. Why would you want to love a woman like that? Fear is what makes people beautiful—at least, it's an ingredient. She has no fear, pal, none whatsoever."

"Why the lecture?"

Packard looked down. "Don't know. Maybe Texas. You're a good guy, you stood with me on that loading dock and helped me gun them down. You didn't waver or shake. That means a lot."

"Yeah, thanks. . . . I don't think I love her. She's just so ungodly beautiful."

A grizzly snicker. "On the outside, pal, just on the outside. On the inside there's not a thimbleful of tenderness. If you need a woman, why don't you just go buy one? You'd be better off. Just go to Vegas, get yourself two of them, three, screw the whole town."

"Maybe I want a family."

A chuckle. "Yep, good luck with that one. You can sit around and tell your kids how you kill people. Here I am, kids, your loving dad, an assassin for the CIA."

"I see it more like being a servant of my country, you know that."

"Sure, sure, but you'll probably end up just tellin' your dog about it, 'cause he'll be the only one who won't ask what being a servant of your country entails. . . . Awe, come on, don't look so sad. That's what this business does, it messes you up. You're not much good when you're done. At least, you wouldn't be to a family."

Tipping his glass up, Bradley swallowed, then looked through the bottom of the glass. It was strange how the bottom of such a small glass could make everything seem so far away. Then he heard Packard's voice again.

"Hey, listen, bub, where're you going for vacation? You're taking one, right? That's what the man said. Take him up on it, do it."

"Maybe," was the glum reply. "I don't know. Maybe I'll go to Atlantic City, play the casinos and stuff."

"Yeah, get yourself a whore, boy."

"Nah."

"Why don't you ask Gretchin to go along, then?"

"Right. God only knows, the woman hates me. Is that not common knowledge? I mean, good gracious, the woman absolutely hates me, give me a break."

Packard took up the bottle and screwed the cap on. "Just ask her," he said. "Take my advice. Just try it. Take it easy, pal." And with that, he left, closing the door quietly behind him.

CHAPTER 7

"Sure," replied Gretchin, keeping her eyes on the watercolor. She had started the picture an hour earlier and now could barely look at it, for all its sloppiness of technique. She had come out in the sunshine and was now perturbed at how everything was gray. She looked up at the darkening sky. "That would be great. Why the hell not?" Then she looked at him. "Close your mouth, Bradley. I'll go."

He checked himself. "I just didn't think you'd say yes. I'm—" he stammered, "I don't know what to say. Except, good, I'm glad, wonderful. And we'll try to get along, okay?"

"Sure. Why the hell not? I'm not usually the problem, am I?"

He gave his head a shake. "Uh, no, no, I guess not. I mean, I guess it's about equal. Listen, I'm sure we can get along."

"So, now you're questioning what I said?"

"No, not at all, I'm just happy you said yes. We can make it work. It'd only be for a month. It's just a vacation, right?"

Looking up at the sky, then down at the picture, she wondered what had ever driven her to go into art in the first place. On-location stuff, with the sun moving the shadows every twenty minutes, drove you insane, and abstraction *was* insane. In representational art you were trying to get inside the body, in abstraction you were trying to get inside the mind, while all around you practically everyone seemed to be looking for happiness by enjoying the outisde of the body and ignoring the mind altogether.

Then she looked at him. "Nothing's *just* anything, Bradley. It's not going to be *just* a vacation. That's lame."

"But you'll go, right? I mean, you'll try, right?"

"I said yes, didn't I?"

Pulling up one of the patio chairs, he sat beside her. He could not help chuckling to himself. Hearing her say yes was a kind of victory. Packard's advice hadn't turned out so badly, after all. Sure he was an old bastard, but not a stupid one.

Then he offered, "That's a nice picture."

Wrinkling her nose, "I'll probably tear it up. It's not what I want, at all. And look at that sky coming in, like bad memories. Yeah, I'll probably tear it up."

"You don't have any bad memories, do you? What bad memories?"

She plunged the brush into the water. "Well, maybe, of shooting a man sitting right beside me in his sports car. Maybe, that, yeah? That's a bad memory, wouldn't you think, *Brad?* Guess you only have good memories."

He shook his head. "No, I have bad memories, too. Sometimes I even have nightmares, and they're pretty awful, which comes with the territory, I guess."

"Yeah, I suppose."

"It's what we do."

"Don't preach at me, Bradley, please don't do that."

"No, but it's all part of the job, isn't it?"

"Sure, but don't talk about it, okay? Don't be a whimp, don't be pathetic."

"But you're always saying I'm pathetic."

"Am I?"

He put his hands together. "So, where do you want to go on the vacation?"

"How should I know? What am I, a travel agent?"

"No, no, you're right, absolutely. I'll pick something out. And I'll ask you about it, okay? . . . How about the shore? Do you like the shore? We could go down to Atlantic City. That would be nice, what do you think?"

She put the brush into the jar, gave it a swish, and then left it there. Untaping the picture, she held it up, closer to her face. Then quickly she tore it in half twice.

"Ah, come on," he protested. "That was nice. I liked it."

"Art's a fucking lie, you know."

"You sound like Connors."

"Yeah, well, Swedes swear, too."

Momentarily he asked, "Do you think she has bad memories?"

"Connors? Good Lord, no, are you kidding? She probably can't sleep at night unless she *has* killed somebody."

"Packard says she's really hard, like, weird. I mean, maybe I shouldn't repeat it, but that's what he said. I think he's just an old stick sometimes, but he has good insight. He could be a genius."

"Hardly. You're easily impressed, bubba. But yeah, he does talk straight."

"Like he shoots."

"Always gotta be the little boy, don't you?"

He chuckled. "So, what about the shore? I think it's a good idea. We could swim."

Leg by leg, she collapsed the easel. "Why not? Let's do it. Wanna leave tomorrow?"

It was not the first time he had found her to be inexplicably adorable. Of course, it was by his own assessment, but wasn't any assessment subjective? Who could make an objective one? Watching her put the brushes into the little box, throw the water out onto the grass, tuck the easel under her arm, he felt a definite pang of lust. Clearly she had evolved past admirable, desirable, to erotic. Yes, fully erotic, with the very cheeks of her ass now visible through the pants. He did not like to use the word *ass,* as it had always seemed lewd or at least crass, but now it seemed perfectly appropriate. He could smell her sweating, feel her sweating as she turned, her breast almost touching his arm, to walk away, and now for some reason he wanted her more than ever.

Before going to his room to pick his clothes out for the trip, he stopped in to see Packard. Although he did not generally take to pathologically antisocial people, he had always found this man to be amiable and open. Besides, the mixed aromas of gun cleaner and whiskey wafting from the room usually worked, he did not know why, like some exotic magnet to draw him.

"Whoa," he said, stopping after taking a step into the room, "what are you drinking in here, gun cleaner or whiskey?"

A grin. "You know you smelled it on the landing, don't pretend, bub. Come on in, close the door, sit down."

The crusty man sat beside his bed, a news-paper-covered table pulled up close, a white rag in one hand and a 686 Smith & Wesson in the other. An old tackle box full of patches, brushes, barrel flashlights, cleaning rods, and other materials lay open before him, like a chest of gold before a crazy old pirate. Beside the box stood an open bottle of Hoppe's Solvent and a smaller, yellowed-plastic squeeze bottle of oil. Finally, an uncapped bottle of Jack Daniel's rested at arm's length.

"I think you're drinking the Hoppe's," said Bradley, taking a seat on the bed. "Or maybe you're going insane just from the vapors.. People do, you know, who breathe that stuff too much."

Packard leaned back in his chair, as if to take a break. "I might as well drink it," he said, running a discolored finger across his upper lip. "I've had it on my skin for most of my life."

"Chemicals are bad."

"What isn't? Besides, if I run out of whiskey, I will drink it, so don't worry about it. What's up?"

"You only clean one gun at a time, right?"

"No, I have four goddamn hands, bub. I clean two at the same time, always. What's up?"

"Just wanted to let you know she took me up on it. We're going to Atlantic City. Leaving tomorrow."

"Hey, great. Buy yourself a box of rubbers and some bourbon and live it up."

"Well, we're just friends."

A show of yellowed teeth. "Yeah, right, friends. I don't know two people in the whole world who hate each other more than you two do."

"Well, why did you suggest it, then?"

Waving a grimy hand, "You'll be fine. Don't worry about it."

"But you suggested it."

"Actually I think both of you are psycho and pretty much deserve each other. But you'll be fine. Sane marriages don't exist."

A frown. "Who's talking about marriage?"

"Not me," said Packard, reaching for the whiskey.

"Why do you drink so much of that stuff? I mean, it's not gun cleaner, but it's still bad."

The soiled hands held the bottle fondly. "You wanna know the truth? I like it."

"Nobody likes it. They drink it for its effect."

Another yellowed smile. "Most do, it seems. But the fact is, I just plain like it. And actually it doesn't have much effect on me. I can probably drink half a bottle and not feel a thing, and a whole bottle without feeling much. it's just the way I am. And I can tell you, I love the stuff."

"Is that why you always smell it before you drink it?"

"Yep. To me, it's beautiful, one of the most wonderful smells on earth. It's like the smell of a woman, there's just something beautiful about it. You don't ask how or why, you just close your eyes and smell it. And on ice, well, that's as close as you can get to the next world."

"Yeah, I see you bringing in the bagged ice."

"It's not like fridge ice, all white and frosty and everything. The bagged stuff, they call it party ice, is pure and makes the whiskey cold, that's all. Jack Daniel's on pure ice, well, there'd better be some in heaven or the first thing I'm gonna do is head out for a drink."

"You and Bobbie Lee, I imagine. She swears by it, too. Whatever."

"Yeah, we both like it."

A wrinkle crept into Bradley's nose as he watched the old man give another sniff at the bottle's top and close his eyes in appreciation. But then he said, "But about marriage, like you were saying, some marriages are pretty good, I think. Some are really nice. Look at Stanley and Martina."

Packard grinned. "But you're just friends, right, bub, like you said? And friendships are sacred, yep."

Nodding, "America's sacred, of course, and football and baseball. And Corvettes are sacred."

Packard pointed the bottle at him, "Guns."

"Yeah, guns. And war too, I guess. But I'm not exactly sure I'd include friendships."

Extending the bottle, "Want a drink, bub? Whiskey's sacred, the holy grail."

"You already made that point, I think. No, thanks. I have to get ready for the trip. See you."

"Take my advice, wash it."

"Yeah, maybe. I'll see."

"Want to shoot some pool after dinner?"

"Sure, one game. I gotta pack."

"And think about the lady."

Pulling the door closed, Bradley replied, "Yeah, and think about the lady, I guess. Sure. ... Hey, that window's not enough. Get a fan going in here. You're going to fall over."

"Doubt it."

It was just after midnight that Stanley returned *I Walk The Line* to its case. Behind him, Martina fluffed her pillow.

"That was a good movie," he said after climbing back into bed. "But the Peck guy was stiff, and she was a little shallow, what do you think?"

Her eyes already closed, she murmured, "Yeah, I think you've got it."

He switched off the light, then turned to her, reaching for her breast. "But they did not show enough of this."

"Typical man, you want a sex movie."

"The Tuesday girl was pretty enough, I am thinking."

"Enough for what?"

"Enough to make me want to see the rest of her."

"Is that what you're thinking?"

"Yes, I am thinking it."

"You're thinking too much, mister. Don't forget, you're touching me, not her."

He had not forgotten. He could never forget what a great gift God had given him in the love of this woman. If he had not found her in his youth but in his prime, still he had found her and now could spend every single day loving her. He had not considered himself lucky in finding her—at least, not too much so. If he admitted there was such a thing as luck, and he often did admit it, still he was keenly aware that finding the love of this woman transcended luck. And embracing her now beneath the sheet, he knew he was embracing not a charm but a gift.

"Do you believe in God?" he asked softly, running a finger around her navel.

"I do," she whispered sleepily. "Why do you ask?"

He chuckled. "*Why do you ask*, you say—is not that funny? Because it is the most important thing in life, could it be otherwise? Life is too frail and too short. Eternity has to be more important than time."

"You're right, I think," she replied, her voice now almost inaudible. "But I am very sleepy. I want to go to sleep in your arms, and I actually don't want to think about eternity, if you don't mind. Just hold me."

From a great distance came the grumbling of an approaching storm, one that according to the weather report was to bring with it a respite of cooler days. She had just drifted off when he slipped out of bed to close the window. His arm coming around her again woke her gently, and she asked him to touch her again in all her favorite places.

The rain was still falling in the morning and put a scowl on Bradley's face. He nearly cursed as he pushed up the umbrella and went to get the Corvette. He considered how he would now be obliged to load up the luggage in the rain. Backing out into the rain, he sat for a moment to listen to the pattering on the roof and to let the wipers clean the windshield. When her red hair suddenly protruded from the front doorway of the Den, he eased the car forward, being extra careful not to splash her. Knowing, however, that she would likely say something critical anyway, he braced himself.

Leaving the umbrella in order to free up both hands, he jumped out. "Okay," he said jovially as he went around to get her travel case, "we're going to put it right behind the seats, so you can get to it, okay?"

Under her umbrella she waited for him to open her door, then said, "Fine, just open it up, okay?"

After putting the case inside, he held the door open for her to get in. As she did he took her arm to steady her. "There we go," he said gently. "Not too bad, huh?" But when she pulled her arm away, exclaiming that she was no old lady, he winced and wished he had not tried to be so courteous. Once back in the driver's seat, he puffed his cheeks and offered, "Boy, I guess we couldn't get sunshine, three lemons, right? Cats and dogs, look at it."

Instantly she fired him a glance of contempt. "Old people say that, Bradley. You're ten years younger than I am, so don't say things like that. Not cool. It's raining, that's all, it's just raining."

Drying the top of his head with a handkerchief, "Sure, Gretchin, okay. So, are you ready to go?"

Incredulous, she replied, "No, I've got to go to the potty, asshole, why do you think I got in the car? You're the one driving, Bradley. Just put the foot down, okay?"

He obeyed and sent the car forward through the slush and down the long driveway. Turning onto the pavement, he lowered the foot even farther. "Hey, here we go. Good ole GM—man, this is a car. Feel that? Puts you back in the seat, doesn't it?" When she did not respond, but sat as if angry or glum, he pacified himself with adjusting the wipers and the air conditioning, and with the odd rush of feeling somehow lucky.

But soon they came upon one of the endemic horse-drawn buggies, and he eased up, blinking impatiently at its red-orange triangle warning of its low speed. He despised things like this, contraptions from the past, though he knew it was not acceptible to be vocal about it. Bringing the Corvette to a crawl, he began to tap the steering wheel and then to groan.

"Patience is a virtue," she said.

When the faces of two children appeared in the buggy's rear window, he murmured, "Come on, people."

"Patience is a virtue," she repeated, but in singsong.

"Hey, old people say that, where's your savvy? Just have to be the school teacher, huh? These Amish are such a pain."

"They're Mennonites, Bradley."

"Same thing. Look at them. I wouldn't take my kids out in something like that, on a two-lane highway, cars and trucks trying to get past you or push you into a ditch. Incredible. Look at those kids' faces. I'd be scared, too. People like that are crazy."

"No, they're just religious. Something wrong with that? You have a problem with that, Bradley? Can't show off in your sports car, huh?"

"They're nuts. Why don't they just walk, get off the road?"

"They're good people, everybody knows that."

"What, and I'm not?"

She looked at him as he still tapped the wheel. Always he had to play the confidence man. True, more than once she had fantasized that he was her lover and pictured herself straddling him in bed, getting what she wanted from him. But that was all she could ever want from him.

"And I'm not?" he repeated.

"No," she answered.

"I go to church," he protested.

"When?"

"I've been a lot. You know that."

"You go there, Bradley. They belong there."

"Well, then, why don't they go where they belong and stay off the road?" Checking his outside mirror, he edged out to pass. "They're in the way, look at them."

"Everybody's in somebody's way, Bradley, get over it."

After again checking to pass, he accelerated and blew past the little buggy, like a wind rushing past a bush in a meadow. "Dumb horse," he muttered. "Now we can get somewhere."

She looked at him again. "You're calling a horse dumb? You, Bradley, really? A horse is one of the smartest creatures on the planet, and you have the nerve to utter something like that?"

Always she knew when and where to hit him. How could he win, with someone like that incessantly trying to punch him out? Life is so weird, he thought, as he pushed the accelerator farther. It bobs and dances in front of you, and no matter how hard you train, it seems always to beat you at the punch, and just before it throws the big one it laughs, for it knows it will always win.

"Awe come on," he blurted, suddenly unable to contain his irritation, "don't start, don't start. Damn it, don't, okay? I do *not* want to hear it."

"Hear what?"

"Anything. Just don't start, I don't want to hear it."

"Like what?" she pushed.

"Okay, okay, like, how smart animals are. They're not smart. Think about it, the horse was doing what they told it to do, not the other way around. You have to admit it. Go ahead, say I'm right."

When they came up behind a semi rig, he floored it and roared past the smoking hulk. The Corvette's power seemed to help make his point. But then he doubted that it would do any such thing, for nothing impressed her, after all.

"If animals needed me to defend them," she said, "I would. But they don't."

"Well, I think those people are weird, that's all. If they don't do the buggy thing, they do the car with the black bumper. I was driving to Harrisburg once and saw one of these little churches with all the buggies outside and over to the side a few cars with black bumpers. And you won't believe it, one of them was a Corvette with black bumpers. A religious Corvette. Too much. I thought I'd die. It was great."

"Yeah," she mocked, "and then you played with your electric train set and went peepee."

"Awe, come on, lay off. Come on, we're gonna have a great time. Seashore, boardwalk, casino, seafood, whatever."

"Uh-huh."

The way she said this made him suddenly want to touch her. He drew his breath, then offered, "I'd really like us to get along better. Maybe we could try not to be so critical of each other."

"What's the matter, Bradley, need a girl? There'll be plenty down there. We're just colleagues, okay?"

"Nothing else, huh?"

Giving him the merest of glances, she replied, "I wouldn't sleep with you, Bradley, if you had the last dick on earth. So, get over it."

"Get over it?"

"Yeah. You know, if you need a girl, go rent one."

"Come on," he said with a groan. "You always have to get crude in a conversation. Can't you ever not get crude? I mean, you know, just talk about things? I'm talking about things, that's all I'm doing. I'm not challenging you or threatening you or anything else. I'm just being normal, that's all, okay?"

"So, you want to be serious, huh? Well, seriously, then, don't you have an old girlfriend you can call? It would be nice if you did, then you wouldn't have to come after me."

He said nothing to this, but then queried, "Why did you agree to go?"

"For the vacation, dope, nothing else."

"You came for the ride?"

"What? Am I supposed to drive myself? Besides, it sounded fun, and I decided on impulse. Listen, don't let it get to you. Think about it, have we ever gotten along, ever?"

"No, I guess not."

"I'm ten years older than you, and yet you were the principal and I was the teacher. I'm sorry to say, I despised you. You were full of yourself, and you're still full of yourself. And you despised me, admit it. Even at the first, as consultants on the team, we couldn't stand each other, and Martina and Maggie knew it. You just have to admit it, we were, and are, the last people on earth who should get together."

Backing off on the accelerator just a little, he said, "Yeah. Yeah, I guess you're right. I guess that's so."

But she said, "So, can you see us sweating in the bed, really?"

Wincing at her candor, he responded only by putting a second hand on the steering wheel. But she noticed it, for she knew he was loathe to do anything that might make him seem less cool. Then she simply turned her gaze upon the trees and the green grass soaking up the rain. Soon they were out on the highway, heading for Atlantic City, and the only thing she could see that interested her was cows in the distance. As the rain began to let up and the countryside to appear refreshed, she asked him to turn off the wipers. She drew a long breath and wondered why she was being driven so fast through a world that was moving so slowly, a world of farming and families, a world she was drawn to. She wondered why she could not just ask him to stop and let her out so that she could walk away from everything and be a part of that slow, meditative world. But life was not like that, she knew. No, life was simply not like that.

Then he began to whistle softly. Suddenly he accelerated and exclaimed, "Man, feel that power!"

Jolted back to herself, she said, "Don't do that, don't yell out like that, and for God's sake don't whistle."

"You never let me whistle. Why not?"

"Because it's puny."

With a shrug, "Okay. . . . Want to hear some music?"

"No. The sooner we get there, the sooner we can come back."

"Oh, so it's gloomy Gretchin now, huh? . . . Listen, I was thinking maybe we could drive through Philly on the way. Nostalgia, kind of. That okay? You're good with that, right?"

"How long did we live there?" she asked rhetorically. "We just left only a few months ago. I mean, God, it's not like an eternity ago or anything. Nostalgia, really?"

Sighing, he replied, "Sure, okay. Forget it."

CHAPTER 8

Milan, Italy, Early September

"Italy is still very hot," Stanley offered, "even in September."

Martina laid her magazine beside her tea. "I do like hot tea, whatever the weather."

"It is not the weather I am talking about," he replied, "it is the temperature." He tipped his orange juice, slurped it, and peered at what was left in the glass. "They always are squeezing it here. It is good, I like it. Everything is good here, except the heat."

"You don't usually complain about things."

"You are correct. And I do not know what is wrong, but there you are having it."

"Just say *there you have it.*"

"Of course. That is exactly what I meant."

"But you *are* complaining."

"Italians should have more ice for the drinks. And more air conditioning."

"Of course," she replied, picking up the magazine. "But it is what it is. And don't slurp, you're not a peasant."

He pointed a finger at her. "I know you, you are vicious. We should go back to bed, and maybe you would not be so vicious."

But then the air began to move around them, and soon a breeze began to cool the sunny table. When she predicted better temperatures for him, he put his head back and looked up at the sky. This was what life was meant to be, he thought, a thing cherished.

"Do you think," she asked suddenly, "that if we live long enough we will be able to forget this work?"

He did not immediately answer. It was good, he thought, to take this vacation. So much of the world they moved in seemed to consist of life-and-death decisions. Reliving those decisions made you sick, at least you felt that way. She was right about the memories.

"No," he finally replied.

"I could have just retired from teaching," she said, "and you from photography, and we would have faced old age with only memories of the love we found."

"You are the romantic."

"I wasn't always."

"I know."

Beyond the planters surrounding the table a little car was being loaded with luggage while a woman tapped her foot impatiently. She began to apply lipstick, then to mutter at the man loading the car. Frantic that he could not fit all the pieces into the car, he eventually stood before her, the remaining travel case in his hands, and announced apologetically that she would have to hold it on her lap. Nervously she got into the car, received the bag from him, then waited for him to get in and drive her.

"She must be his wife," said Martina.

"Yes, and now she will beat him to death with her words."

"We're not all like her, you know."

"No," he replied, his eyes upon the little car as it drove away, "and we are not all like him. It is fortunate, yes?"

"Do you think you would win, Mr. Osipov, in the battle of the sexes, or do you simply fear that I would?"

"You would win," he replied softly, "but it is a battle in which the winner only seems to win."

"Don't relish it?"

"I need a lover, not a competitor. In that battle nobody ever really wins. I am glad we have not taken it up."

Once more she lifted the magazine. "I am happy that Maggie wanted to stay and look after things. I hope she enjoys Leonard's company."

He ran a finger around the inside rim of the glass, then put the finger into his mouth to lick off the orange juice pulp. "Yes," he said, "it would be good to have ice in my juice. But in this heat it would not last long."

"Do you think our love will last?"

"No," he answered without looking at her. It was the truth, but he did not want to look at her as he said it. "I love you now. But, no—the answer must be no. If I had ice in this glass, it would improve the drink, but it would melt. I have never seen human love that lasts. It is a fact of life that almost invariably it will not. Intentional love, yes, but being in love, no. Being in love seems to be an option everybody wants but nobody can choose. . . . We did not choose it."

"No," she said softly, "we did not."

"But it is nice."

"Yes," she said, "it is very nice. But I will not be surprised if it goes the way of your ice, Mr. Osipov."

"The ice I wanted but could not have. In this heat, it would not have lasted long anyway."

"Hopefully our love will be less ephemeral. Eventually it will falter. But we have until then, yes?"

"Yes," he replied, now looking at her. "Yes, we have until then."

Then she dropped her eyes in an attempt to immerse herself in the article she had intended that morning to read. But as her eyes moved across the words images came to her of the Russian contact he had shot in the head with his Makarov—the woman's grotesque expression, her red death chair blackened with her blood, and the way he stood over her, grasping the gun. Often she had seen this husband of hers, this Stanley Osipov, this man she had married, wield a camera, but she had not until that night seen him wield a deadly weapon. That was the night of the team's real beginning, and it was her husband, this man she now wished to be in love with forever, who had fired the christening shots. The images that belonged to that night, she knew, would be forever with her, even longer perhaps than her love for him. But now she heard his voice from across the table.

"We should take the boat to Varenna," he said, meeting her eyes. "I would like to walk again the same streets."

"You are being nostalgic."

"Yes, I am," he replied. "We have much to remember . . . and much to look forward to."

She smiled at him. "We can eat there in the afternoon and come back tonight. It will be beautiful, and we will both remember."

Later, when their boat moved away from the platform and began to make its way toward Varenna, they watched together the reflections of the town in the water as they left it. When they took a seat to enjoy the open water and the open sky they did not speak of their love or even of their work for the Agency, but only of each other.

"You need," he offered at length, "to be letting me into your thoughts more. I want to be more inside your thoughts."

"Then you'll have to guess those thoughts," she returned.

"I am not good at guessing," he complained.

"Then you'll have to learn to read my mind."

"As in a crystal ball."

"Yes."

"But I am thinking that I read your mind now. I often know what you are going to do. But I did not mean that, at all. I meant your thoughts, your personal thoughts."

"Why do you want to be inside my thoughts?"

"Because," he replied, "I want to be there when I die."

She made no reply, but simply watched the lake, wondering how deep it was and whether moving into eternity would be like moving across such waters.

"You are thinking now," he said. "What are you thinking?"

"Gloomy things."

"Then I want to know about those things."

"Do you think," she queried at length, "we will grow old rapidly or slowly?"

He put his hands together. "If we are to be growing old, we will, I think, be growing old slowly. We are pretty healthy, you must be admitting."

"Yes," she laughed. "Yes, we are. I am seventy-one and you are sixty-one, but yes, we are pretty healthy."

He leaned close. "At least, we were this morning."

"You don't want inside my thoughts, you want inside my body. They say that one thing and one thing only is on a man's mind—sex."

"I do not think about it all the time," he protested. "That would be terrible. It would leave no time for mystical thoughts."

She shook her head, as if reluctant to respond to his levity. "What is your favorite dish?"

"You are changing the subject. My favorite thing to eat, as you have full well knowledge of, is steak."

"God, you need to work on your English, mister Moscow."

That night, after returning from Varenna, they took a shower together and then lay quiet in each other's arms upon their bed. Then he reached over and turned out the light, so they could go into the darkness together.

"We are," she offered, "in each other's thoughts now, I think."

"It is so beautiful to be without clothes. Maybe not in Siberia, but here, yes." Then he kissed her nipples and her belly.

"Italy will always be a special place for us. We'll come back every year, if we can, until we are too old to come back . . . too old to come back."

"But we will grow old slowly and come back often, yes."

"Yes," she whispered.

Lancaster County

"Do you like dogs, Len?" Maggie asked as Helga, the mighty German Shepherd, and Tai Ping, the fearsome Jindo-Chow, raced and played and then ran themselves out of sight.

Packard, who had joined her for the patio lunch, dragged a chair from the table and sat down. "I do," he replied. "I like most things that are powerful. Unless they're threatening me, of course."

"Of course," she agreed.

"These dogs are okay by me, though. They can guard me any time they want. I'll even teach them to drink. Yeah, I like powerful things."

"Such as guns."

"Yep."

He liked her. She had caught his eye the first time he saw her as she entered the classroom where Kessler had set up for the negotiation. She had seemed aloof, but he had looked anyway.

"You certainly seem to," she returned. "And not just as tools, but more as friends."

"You got it, lady."

"You know," she said, "The first time I saw you, I was a little frightened of you." She gave him a moment to respond to this, but as he did not, she continued, "That day in the classroom. You were slouched in your chair and your coat was crumpled up. You wore a scowl on your face, as if scowling was all you ever did. Remember?"

"The classroom, sure. The coat—I usually wear some kind of coat, so what's the difference? The scowl, no, I don't remember, I'm afraid not. But I'm sure you're right, people have told me I have a serious look. So, you're right, of course. . . . I do remember seeing you, though."

She felt herself flush, but then turned away and said, "The dogs seem to like you, especially Ping. He hides out in your room sometimes, doesn't he?"

"Yeah, he's there. I guess the solvent fumes don't bother him."

"Nor those of the whiskey," she added, handing him the bowl of potato salad she had prepared.

From the first, she had found him odd. It was not a negative oddness, but one nevertheless. Always he seemed to prefer sitting alone. And the guns, those two big guns, always holstered ominously under his arms. And quiet—God, was he quiet, like some killer monk. The strangest man, and yet, not unattractive, not at all. The stubbled chin, the gritty look. If she had not care to think of the blood he had shed, she would admit under duress perhaps that she had often thought of him, for the man that he so obviously was. She looked at him now, the gaunt, mechanically grim eyes, the wolf-like aura. Even now as she handed the bread also she was aware of the blood ink of him in her mind.

Taking a slice of the bread, he queried, "Did you bake this?"

"Yes, I did. I hope you like it."

"I smelled it baking this morning. Drove me crazy, almost made me come looking for it."

She did not bother to hide her pleasure at the compliment. "Well, thank you, Len."

"You're welcome, Maggie."

It was rare to hear him address anyone, especially a woman, by her first name. "You don't usually call me that."

Producing a sulfur-colored smile, he asked, "What do I call you?"

"You don't, actually."

He took a bite of the bread. "Guess you're saying I'm unfriendly. Guess you're right."

"No, no," she returned, "not at all, Len. It's just that, well . . . yeah, maybe a little." When he did not reply, she asked, "Have you ever been psychoanalyzed?"

His surprise at the question put a growl in his tone. "Hell no! Jesus!"

"You might benefit from it, you know."

Taking another bite of the bread, he nodded toward the dogs, who had returned and were encircling the table, sniffing at the food. "Would you analyze them? Do you think it would benefit them or anyone else?"

"Of course not," she answered sweetly. "They're okay the way they are. But people are more finely tuned, don't you think? You know, like Ferraries compared to Fords."

"Nice analogy, lady. But no, I'll pass. I know what psychoanalysis would find, and it wouldn't be good."

Then she just handed him the butter and contented herself with the silence and occasionally watching him eat. She had not thought too much as to why she enjoyed watching people eat and drink. Once, when she was in Paris, she had occupied herself with the activity for an hour with half a sandwich and a small bottle of wine at a sidewalk table. At first it seemed exquisitely sensuous, while in the end it nearly offended her, especially after a man in a suit dribbled tomato soup onto his white shirt.

Suddenly he blurted, "You're a good cook, like I've said before."

"You have complimented me a few times, Len, yes. Thank you, I'm glad you like it."

Then he fell silent and simply looked at her. When she noticed, he told her she wielded a hell of a .38. Then unconsciously he extracted one of his Smiths and laid it beside his plate. It was something he did occasionally to help his digestion.

Amused, she queried, "Did you ever have one of those go off accidentally?"

"Nope. . . . Well, I guess I did, a semi-auto. I was fooling around with it. But not one of these."

Although she had known him now for some time and had observed him in both casual and dangerous situations, still she found it almost bewildering how cold he could be, not as to his emotions, but his intellect. And more, it was as if he knew this about himself but simply didn't care.

Then she found herself asking, "Did anyone ever accuse you of being antisocial?"

"Oh, sure," he replied. "Hell, they called me that in high school, probably in grade school."

"Oh, okay. So, you weren't offended?"

"Nah, I'm a sociopath if I ever met one, that's for sure. But I wouldn't hurt anybody, I'm harmless."

"Yes, yes, of course."

Leaning back in his chair, he hooked a thumb comfortably around a strap of the jackass rig. Contentedly he said, "Ah, it's a fine day, don't you think, Maggie?"

"Yes," she replied, her eyes traveling from the old sport coat, which barely covered the butt of his other Smith, to the pinstripe shirt, which glowed stark against the cross strap of the holsters, "yes, it is, Len, a beautiful day." Then giving her head a shake, as if to clear her thoughts, she said, "How ... how about a movie this evening, what would you say to that?"

He picked up the magnum and shoved it back into its holster. "Why the hell not? What're you going to watch?"

"Well, I have a number of possibilities actually. I'll bring a few down and let you pick one out."

His eyes moved over her hair, then her face, her eyes, her lips, then came to rest on her blouse. He imagined the shape of the breasts. He liked skinny women. It wasn't that he didn't enjoy looking at a curvy woman, not at all. But around the skinny ones his heart raced. Preferences aside, of course, he found women to be pleasant to think about, but difficult to converse with. And he didn't care what they wore, for God's sake. The object was to get their clothes off, not to stand around telling them how nice they looked. Sure there was more to it than that, but not much more. About ninety percent of the female world, he figured, deserved nothing but contempt.

Finally he rasped his reply. "Sure."

Clearing her throat, she said pleasantly, "You forgot to add *why the hell not.*"

Standing before the mirror, she began to wonder why she had fantasized about sleeping with this man. Did she really want a killer climbing all over her? But perhaps he was not a climber. And what could any of it matter anyway? Considering the body before her, it was obvious that the exercise and discipline had been a good investment. The genetics hadn't hurt, of course, but the extra tredmill work over the years had added some muscle to the trim figure. Suddenly uncomfortable with observing her skin, she went to the dresser and chose a soft cotton top. She would show, of course, but at her age every thing helped, at least in theory.

He was waiting for her, a glass of whiskey in his hand, as she entered the recreation room. She did not meet his gaze, but simply spread the movies before him on the coffee table.

"Well, I have three I thought you might like," she said cheerily. "But I have more, if these aren't good."

Averting his gaze from her protruding nipples, he took in a little of the whiskey and let it roll around his tongue. "Want a drink?"

"Yes, that would be good. We have some gin, don't we? But you're not looking at the movies. How about *Seabiscuit?* This is nice, I think you'd like this one."

"How do you know I haven't seen it?"

"You don't strike me as a movie watcher. But you must like horses, or tell me if I'm wrong. I guessed you might like horse racing, yes?"

With a shrug, "Sure, sounds good. Let's watch it."

"Not so fast, there. Patience is—"

"Don't say it, please," he broke in, lifting the glass and giving the whiskey a slurp. "Besides, I have no virtues, I'm afraid. Listen, let me get that gin for you. Want ice?"

"Yes, please. But now you have to choose our movie."

"The horse movie's fine. Put it on."

"No, no," she said, touching his arm, "you have to choose. I also have *Out Of Africa* and *The English Patient.* What do you think?"

"How the hell should I know, I haven't seen any of 'em, what're they, chick flicks? The horse movie'll do. Let me get that gin."

"Would you like popcorn? I can pop it up in a second."

Throwing her an affirmative nod, with a glance at the nipples, he left the room.

CHAPTER 9

Cape May, New Jersey

As the SUV topped the bridge and began its descent into Cape May Connors took her eyes from the traffic to catch the harbor at dusk. All seemed tinted lavender, as though the ghost of a purple cat was returning to haunt the docks.

"Hungry?" she queried.

Bobbie Lee, who had been snoozing for the last ten minutes, blinked and then raised her head from the pillow she had lodged against the glass. "Well," she drawled, "hungry or not, we'd jist better pull in. We were told."

Smirking at this, Connors wheeled them into the parking lot of the Lucky Bones Restaurant. "T'ink we're supposed to eat here or across the straet. Both places, she said, were fuckin' good."

"Jist *good*, I think, from Martina, she's a lady. Look, expensive cars. Bunch of richies, I'd say. Look right there, a Maserati. You don't see many of them in Tinnessee, I can tell you. Hey, we prob'ly wouldn't have to lock up here, richies never try to get in your car."

Connors got out, slinging Stanley's D80 over her shoulder. "Maybe not," she returned, "but ef somebody gats en, they'll see we're carryin' enough ammo to blow up Parliament."

"Oh, yeah, Guy Fawkes. I've heard of that. That was some IRA cowboy that did that, wasn't it?"

Giving her key a squeeze, Connors sent the solenoids home. "Hardly. He was from York, not Cork. Brits don't need the Irish to blow 'am up, they joost do et thamsalves."

"Come on, now, be sweet."

After they were led to a spacious booth by a window, Bobbie Lee rolled her eyes. "Talk about lucky. A booth. No little table for us, even with all these people here. Shit, that's lucky."

Early the next morning they opened the blinds and looked out upon a blue sunlit ocean. For a moment they stood silent, stunned by the intensity of the brilliant scene. Up and down the simple beach people walked or jogged while above them seagulls rose in the breezes and in the distance little boats made their way along the coast.

"Gorgeous," said Bobbie Lee softly.

"Me dad took us to the sea once."

"Well, don't get pathetic on me. You need to fergit stuff. You'll live longer. Anxiety'll kill you pretty efficiently."

"You're roight."

"Seafood, that's what we need."

A shrug. "Lat's walk the beach, then gat an early lunch, how's about t'at?

"Sure, let's do it. Exercise, a beauty walk, yep."

The sun was at its zenith when they took lunch under an umbrella at the docks. An old schooner whose deck had been fitted out as a quaint restaurant slept not far from their table, the placid waters of the harbor gently lapping its barnacled planks. Screeching seagulls fluttered upon nearby piling, waiting for them to finish and be foolish enough to leave a shrimp or two behind.

As one white gull glided in a wide circle just above the schooner's masts, Connors pressed her back against the plastic rungs of her chair and watched him. Suddenly the gull dropped into a brief freefall, then fluttered down to rest upon a nearby post. It was funny, she considered, how nature often came so close to you that you felt you could reach out and touch its beauty. And sometimes that beauty was so exquisite that it made you think of heaven. The gull, cocking his head to consider her, lifted a wing delicately. As she looked back at him she felt that it would not take much to coax her from this earth. Then she heard Bobbie Lee's voice.

"They're like angels, I guess. I can't keep from lookin' at 'em, either." Scratching her nose and then dipping a shrimp into a ketchup tub, she said, "It's good I did the orderin'—they wouldn't have understood a word you said."

"You're not much batter. Fuckin' heck."

"Ah, come on, it's not *heck,* it's *hick.* You can do it, you can say it, jist try."

"How about joost *radnack*?"

With a glare, "Goddamn IRA—always spoilin' fer a fight. Well, I ain't accommodatin' you, I'm gonna enjoy my shrimp."

From an outbound yacht just making its way past the schooner came a sudden horn blast, and they turned to see laughing people waving from its canopied rear deck. Women clad in bikinis and shirtless men clad in shorts stood holding bottles of beer. The entire party seemed well on their way to intoxication.

Bobbie Lee, depositing a shrimp tail at the corner of her platter carton, gave a quick sniff and said, "They can drink and screw, but its too cold to swim."

Connors, who had been thinking that the revelers were like curios in a museum, simply said, "Ded you ever t'ink how easy et es to pull a tregger?"

Dipping a french-fry into ketchup, "I have thought of that, girl, yep. It's ridiculously easy."

Cape May Point Bird Sanctuary
As the SUV rolled across the parking lot and moved into a space by the observation platform the number of groups of birds flying in close proximity seemed to increase. Lowering a window, Connors watched as a flock glided past and headed for a line of birdhouses. She then shifted her gaze to a motley group of birders laden with spotting equipment and lumbering up the ramp of the observation platform.

"The pamphlet," she said, "gives all the kinds of birds. You can't count all the kinds. How do t'ese people learn t'is stuff?"

"Well, that's what we're supposed to be doin' here, bein' birders, so git over it. Look at that lighthouse. I love lighthouses, but I'm always thinkin' they're gonna fall over. Guess I thought that when I was a kid, ain't that funny? But look at that thing, ain't it amazin'?"

"Et's joost a fuckin' loighthouse. Want me to take pectures or somet'in'?"

"You're jist a killjoy, girl. . . . Let's take a walk over to that observation thing. But this place is too public. Might as well kill somebody on TV."

"Aye, koind of waird."

At the platform they chose the ramp and soon stood at the edge of a group of about thirty spotters. Tripods were everywhere, most topped with huge lenses, their owners inviting anybody who came near to take a look. A woman in a green canvas hat announced she had her lens fixed upon a nest across the first lake. The man next to her said his was trained upon a family of swans, if anybody wished to take a look. Apparently not many of the fellow birders or visiting tourists did.

Popping the lens cover from her camera, Bobbie Lee began to move slowly through the chatting crowd, with Connors following suit. After checking out the people, they took the steps instead of the ramp and returned, under a swarm of seagulls, to the SUV.

Bobbie Lee tossed her sunglasses onto the dash. "She might be out on one of the trails. And she might be at one of the bird lakes."

"Ever swem en the ocean?"

"Sure. You?"

"No."

"Well, it's too cold here. Try it in the summer sometime, girl."

"Loife's a fuckin' trep, esn't et?"

"Trip? Yeah, sure. . . . What's wrong?"

"Joost t'inkin'."

A sigh. "This is pritty simple. We're supposed to be here takin' pictures of birds, killin' somebody, an' enjoyin' the scenery. No big deal. It's practically a vacation, and then we git to go on vacation when we git back. That's two vacations, girl, what more could you want?"

"I know."

"Lord. Listen, wanna play min'ature golf? Ever do that? We passed a cute min'ature golf course on the way, right on the main strip. C'mon, let's go, what say?" When there was no response, she said, "Jist put down your gun and relax, girl. Can you relax or not?"

"Sher."

Bobbie Lee turned the key, put her sunglasses on, and said, "I hate sad people. And it seems like the Irish are sad a lot. Maybe that's why you people drink."

Then Connor's phone chimed. "It's Kassler." She took her time in answering. "Yeah. . . . Yeah. . . . No, haven't. Haven't been lookin' too hard. Want us to start? . . . Sher. . . . Yeah, she's okay, she's sattin' roight here. . . . Sher. . . . G'boye." Then she closed the phone and snickered, as though she had been talking to a fool.

When they had reached the highway and were heading away from the Point, Bobbie Lee said, "I don't really know how he understood you. Your Irish lingo sounded practic'ly backwater. What'd he say?"

"He said not to look for her, but joost to relax and wait for her to show up. He said to take en the soites."

"There you go. It's *sites.* You can do it if you work at it. Hell, you'd sound real good, even a little American, if you tried, girl."

"He said everybody goes to watch the sunset at the end of the main drag."

Pointing to her right, Bobbie Lee lightly touched the brake. "That's some of the sanctuary over there. Ain't it jist real pritty?"

"Et's noice."

"Listen, if we do the sunset thing, we won't have time for min'ature golf. There won't be time if we go to dinner too, and I'm real hungry."

"You're too skenny to eat as much as you do."

"I've gotta eat for energy to grow my tits."

"Tets're made of fat."

"Not mine. They're muscle, which comes from liftin' weights. I'm wirey, and I drink a lot. I guess we'd better check out the sunset thing. They might show up. Okay, we'd better skip the golf. But not dinner, I need the dinner."

Connors closed her eyes and put her head back. "I don't fuckin' care. Joost droive."

Sunset Point

Following dinner, they stopped for salt water taffy, then drove to the end of the strip. A massive sun, hovering ominously over the ocean at the horizon, seemed noticeably to be dropping as they parked, got out, and made their way toward the pavilion at Sunset Point. Although the crowd that had gathered seemed mostly to consist of tourists, many of the birders encountered earlier at the lookout platform were among them. In the ethereal light the sound of camera shutters being clicked seemed to be nearly as constant as that of the soft waves rolling in upon the nearby sand. Across the water, at Cape May Point, both the lighthouse and the setting sun seemed to be competing for the part of main actor in the glorious scene.

Slinging their cameras, they moved quietly through the crowd. At the beach, they turned to make their way back to the pavilion. When Connors suddenly stiffened, then stopped, Bobbie Lee stopped also. Casually they turned and snapped pictures of the sunset. But as Bobbie Lee looked around she too saw the woman, their target, among the ccrowd. With her were a female companion and two Slavic-looking men standing close behind. The two women, dressed in linen pants and windbreakers, cooed excessively over how beautiful the sky had grown, whereas the men, in jeans and windbreakers, stood silent, their faces expressionless, their eyes watchful.

When they had returned to the SUV, Connors, pulling her door shut, groaned aloud. The crowd were still watching as the final sinking of the sun lit up the horizon.

"Well, they dedn't tell us about t'es," she said. "T'ose were bodyguards, tough as shet. Now et's four of 'am."

Bobbie Lee tossed her cap onto the dash. "They looked like pros to me. Eastern European, or something. Wouldn't wanna run into 'em at the dumpster when I was taking the trash out, that's fer sure."

"You're roight, there. Romanian or some such. Gunmen. Maybe we should joost go play fuckin' golf."

"I detect sarcasm, and I'm not sure I like it. Min'ature golf's a good game. It's funner than jist about anything, and it's so goddamn clean you could play it on Sunday."

Ignoring this, Connors pulled out her phone. "I'd batter call Kassler, 'cause we're gonna have to kell the guards to gat to her."

Cheerily, "But it's not a big deal if we do. Shit, I could've killed her right back there, shot her in the head, *and* her chick, right there, and jist kept on walkin'. Jist like that, and the whole rodeo would have been entirely over. But I ain't shootin' four of 'em in a crowd. No way." Removing the top from the box of taffy, she selected a yellow piece, unwrapped it, and put it into her mouth. "You want a pink one? I don't think I'm gonna like the pinks. Ever' time I git a piece of candy that's pink, it tastes like toothpaste, and I ain't eatin' toothpaste."

But Connors' eyes were on the people. "The crowd's breakin' up now. They'll be comin' back weth the crowd. They're gonna pass us. See which car they gat en."

"I like taffy," remarked Bobbie Lee, smacking her lips with pleasure, "but I hate toothpaste. Ever have whiskey after brushin' your teeth? It's pritty bad, let me tell you, I can swear right now, 'cause it's still in my mem'ry."

"They're gattin' en the Laxus. All four of 'am. Good. Not sher I'd wanna run down two cars."

"Damn!" exclaimed Bobbie Lee, sliding the selector to Reverse. "It would've bin so easy, and colorful too—a beachful of birders, the sun goin' down real beautiful and all. Hell, Merry goddamn Christmas, jist like a movie."

They followed the Lexus to Cape May's only mall, a quaint area with a cobblestone walkway that ran between pretty tourist shops. They waited until the car parked and the four got out.

"Don't tell me," muttered Bobbie Lee in a disgusted tone, "they're gonna shop. Okay, my luck. Wanna follow 'em around the strip mall? God, this place is nice. People've got money here, I can promise you that. When I was a kid I threw rocks at rich people. Now I jist appreciate them."

Connors looked at her, then said, "Joost pull en somewhere. Lat's talk."

Finding a spot, Bobbie Lee switched the engine off. "If we follow them around a little bit, we can git some ice cream, maybe some coffee."

For a moment neither spoke. Then Connors said, "Ded et ever occur to you t'at Kassler's tryin' to gat us kelled?"

Silence, then, "Where'd that come from, girl?"

"I'm askin', t'at's all. Ded et occur to you, or not?"

"Uh—no—not really."

"Et's t'at t'eory."

"*His* theory?"

"Yeah."

"Hm. Well, actually I think it's kind of amusin'. What we know of it, anyway. You're sayin' there's more to it, I guess."

" 'Course there es. Have to be bloind to mess et."

Momentarily, "Correct me, but my understandin' is that he simply wants to prove that untrained people can make better agents than trained ones. What's wrong with that? I kind of agree with him. Trainin' can really make a stooge out of you. I'm not trained. I worked with the police, an' all, but I'm not trained. And you're jist a paid killer, or whatever you are. I mean, we're pros, like Len, but none of us are trained. The others were school teachers. Even the twit was a principal—I guess that's redundant. And we're pritty good as a team, I think, so what's your beef with that?"

"Not t'at part, et's the rast of et."

With a sigh, "Okay. Why don't you jist spill what's botherin' you? Here we are, dark car, an' all, all secret, an' all, nobody listenin'. The shitheads are shoppin' or maybe even havin' ice cream and coffee, which, I would remind you, *we* are not. But go ahead, say what's on your mind."

"Et may not be his t'eory, but his plan es to gat us wacked when he's done weth us. Et's obvious. Martina and Osipov see et. Maggie too, far as I know."

Following a moment of consideration, Bobbie Lee unwrapped another taffy and said, "Okay, so what? Actually it kind of makes sense. . . . What're they supposed to do, retire us, turn us loose, give us all a free life membership at a movie complex and say *go count your wrinkles*?"

Connors stared at her. "No, 'course not. But he's proven his t'eory, whech es why the Agency's so happy weth us, the data's there. Now et's toime to gat rid of us, for the fuckin' money's sake, ef nothin' alse. Fuckin' downturn and all t'at. Cuttin' carners."

"You're sayin' he knew about the bodyguards, didn't tell us, and jist let it happen."

A nod. "He ded."

"What're you gonna say when you call?" After there was no response and she had watched as the colorless eyes, eerily reflecting the ambient street light, worked from side to side, she said, "I'm askin' you here, girl."

Connors then answered, "I'm not goin' to call hem. I t'ink we should joost kell the four of 'am and then tell hem."

"But next time there'll be eight or ten. He's jist gonna try harder next time, if what you're sayin' is true, and I believe you, girl. I mean, it looks right to me. Shit, I think you're right. Why not jist tell him right on the goddamn phone—jist pick it up and tell him, right there and see what he does? Why not? You know, take the offinsive and all."

"Because I don't want to put t'at koind of power en his hands roight now. We stell have to do the job, and I want him behind us to a caertain extant. Besoides, I wanna t'ink about et."

"What's to think about?"

"How to fuckin' do him."

"Kill Kessler?"

"No, his fuckin' mother, moron."

Bobbie Lee replaced the box lid. "Killy, that's big. You'd do that?"

"Wouldn't try to. Wouldn't walk up on his parch and do et, but ef he walked up on moine, I would."

Recalling the porch scene, she said, "Yeah, and then go where, Antarctica? Nobody beats the Agency. Nobody ever beat the KGB either, ask Stanley about that one, girl. You put a bullet in Kissler's head, and they'll come fer you right quick. Killin' an agent's serious, real serious. It's worse'n gittin' a pink taffy, I can tellya that."

Connors looked out into the night, as though it was the ocean. There was nothing to think or be or want, beyond the endlessness of the ocean and its cold, dark, eternal nothingness. But this did not make her sad, for nothing had ever really promised to make her happy. Then she saw a man and woman walking toward the strip mall. Apparently spontaneously they took each other's hand and then put an arm around each other's waist. It was not something she ever expected to have for herself. But again, life was like that, she thought, ever presenting the sensitive, the beautiful, just beyond reach. Then she heard herself answering, "I'd prob'ly joost go back to me moother. Sattle down, gat a dog. Lat 'am come and gat me, lat 'am come and foind me."

"Your father was IRA, wasn't he?"

"Whole fuckin' fam'ly was. Lat the Agency foind me there among the Army, lat 'am look, the stupid bastards. You t'ink the Agency's tough? I swear to

Mary, the Army's tougher, or at least a whole fuckin' lot meaner."

"Think they'd understand me in Irelan'?"

"Give me a taffy." Then, "Prob'ly not, fuckin' heck."

"That's *hick,* girl, git it straight. . . . Well, if you ever put Kissler down, I might go with you. Think there'd be room?"

"Might be. But the people I know don't play min'ature golf. They joost drenk and kell people, loike I do."

"Sounds like a beautiful life. Maybe you'd like Tinnessee. It's real nice in Tinnessee. Ever'body jist drinks, screws, and decorates their front yard with old junk cars. It's real nice. You'd like it there."

"Sounds loike a fantasy world you're trying to sell me. T'is es modern America, for fuck's sake. Besides, et's too hot there."

"It is hot, I'll grant you that, you make a good point. That's why we always drink our sour mash on ice there."

CHAPTER 10

Unhappy, Connors pulled at the bill of her cap. "Slow fuckers," she muttered as a jovial family finished up at the first hole. Tapping the rubber grip of her putter upon the synthetic turf, she watched as Bobbie Lee filled in their names on the score card.

"You're holdin' that like it's a gun. Calm down, this is gonna be fun. Min'ature golf is one of them better-'n-sex things."

"Only wheskey's batter'n sax, and I don't gat much of either."

"We'll have to address that some other time. Try to focus, girl."

"I need a drenk."

"Let's go, it's our turn. And here's some taffy."

Unwrapping the candy, Connors said with a grin, "Here we are, playin' golf an' eatin' sweets, instead of out makin' a difference."

"I love that, very funny. You mean, out reducin' the population, I think. Now watch, this is how it's done." She placed the ball, then tapped it forward. "And the object, obviously, is to have a bunch of fun, slow the clock down."

Later, strolling Cape May's modest boardwalk, they took in the shops, bought more taffy, and stopped for lunch at an open-air restaurant. In the distance, the mild surf rolled in its sea scent to fill the breeze that blew around their table.

"This food," declared Bobbie Lee over the shrimp salads they had ordered, "might even compete with min'ature golf."

"Only a Protestant would say somet'in' loike t'at."

Benevolently, "That wasn't necessary, not one bit necessary. Catholics are nuts, bunch of statue kissers, so don't talk to me. What're your prayers like, girl?"

"I say the rosary."

A smirk. "I can see you countin' bullets, but not beads."

"You come to Ireland, the alves'll gat you."

"I might could believe in Mary a little bit, but maybe not elves, no way. Tinnessee's heaven anyway, that's where life begins and inds. You can walk out your door and empty your magnum in your own back yard, without nobody thinkin' nothin' about it. They'd prob'ly hang you in Irelan' jist fer ownin' a gun."

"Ever'body carries one anyway. Some priests even carry one."

"Tell you what, it's real sweet in Tinnessee. You want priests? We've got priests in Tinnessee, right in Mimphis, nuns too. There's religion all over the place there. You come on down."

"Too hot."

"It ain't that hot, and it's greener than Irelan', I'll guarantee it. You git up in the mornin' an' see that Confederate flag a-hangin' from the porch, your heart pumps like a Harley. There ain't nothin' like it."

"Are you sher you're not Irish?"

"Welsh, I think."

"I'm joost wonderin' how I'm gonna gat you ento Sinn Fein. They'll prob'ly call you a slave runner and keck your ass."

Bobbie Lee looked away for a moment. "Don't git me started. The Civil War wasn't about slavery. Didn't know that, did you? The Brits stopped slavery years before America did, and without a civil war. If there hadn't been a Civil War in America, the South would've stopped slavery on their own, and they would've done it in the right way and at the right time. They would've transitioned it in prob'ly jist a few years. But the North wouldn't have it, hell no, jist had to push and push 'till the South fired on Sumpter. You think the North cared about the slaves? No way. The Civil War wasn't about slavery, it was about the opposite, it was about freedom. It was really about a culture, a way of life. Now, that *is* worth a war, in my opinion."

"So, the South cared about the slaves?"

"Hell no. They cared about their own honor, that's all, their own way of life, their indepindence, their culture, their name. They were selfish as shit, jist like you and me. Tell me you're not selfish as shit, go ahead, jist tell me, and say it with a straight face, like Mary's listenin'. Tell me the slaves weren't selfish as shit. What were they, a buncha goddamn saints? They were jist like the Southerners and the Yankees, jist human, that's all. They were marketed into the equation, that's all."

"Sounds loike the Irish."

"Yeah, you people've got your own Yankees, ain'tcha? And your war's about the same thing as ours. It sure ain't about the goddamn issues, it's about honor, culture, a way of life, and you know it."

Lifting her glass, Connors looked through its water. "I've haerd Southerners can foight."

"We can. Prob'ly because a lot of us are Irish. We fight like the Irish, only we don't git as drunk. We squabble pritty much all the time. We do people fights, dog fights, cockfights, it doesn't matter, even motorcycle fights an' car fights. Hell, most of the U.S. military is made up of Southerners, prob'ly. We were in Vietnam, all the wars. In the Civil War, the North lost 360,000 men, but the South only 250,000. Southern boys can be real mean, like dog shit for breakfast. Gittin' called a redneck's like receivin' a badge of honor. We love it."

"They sound loike some people I know."

"Hey, me and you's got a lot in common. We should stick togither, girl. Maybe somebody'll pay us to fight some war."

"Maybe we're foightin' et now."

A chuckle. "I think you're right." Then she looked into the colorless eyes, enough to see the blue ocean reflected in them. At length she said, "It's time we left, I think. You ready?"

"Yeah, why not?"

"Don't be negative, girl," said Bobbie Lee, reaching for her wallet to pay the tip, "there's stuff to do. And the ozone's gittin' thinner every day."

The lot was nearly empty when they arrived at the sanctuary. Although the Lexus was not there, they climbed the platform to check out a small group gathered with cameras and spotting scopes, then took one of the observation trails to the lakes. When they encountered a man and woman decked in birding gear Bobbie Lee offered a *hey y'all,* but Connors, only a silent stare. At the third lake they stopped to watch the families of ducks and swans resting or paddling in the cool water and the myriads of birds gliding through the warm air.

"Now, this, is real pritty, look at this," said Bobbie Lee, taking a deep breath. "I love nature, it's jist so nice."

"Ded you ever hunt?"

After spitting into the water, "Not animals, that's fer sure. I hate hunters worse'n Yankees. Did you ever hunt?" And when the other merely shook her head and pushed her camera out of the way, "You can activate the shutter like that."

Connors grinned. "Sorry, yeah, et's not the kind of tregger I'm used to."

"You know your birds at all?"

"No. . . . Lat's cross the dunes, take a look at the beach."

As they reached the crest of the dunes they noted that the stretch of sand connecting Sunset Beach and the lighthouse was nearly devoid of people. The great mounds, covered with grass and bushes, lay like a wall to protect the sanctuary.

Descending to the ocean side, they made their way in the direction of the light surf.

"What's the logic in leavin' that hulk there, I wonder," remarked Bobbie Lee. "Lord, that thing's ugly. Somebody should jist blow it up."

"The brochure said et was built to spot an envasion. They must've really been stupid. Et's all concrete. I t'ink they've laft et here for the tourists. As ef tourists would ever want to look at et."

"Not many people out here. ... See them people on the ramp? Let's take that way back. I'm gittin' kind of tired lookin' at noth—" She did not finish, for among the group could now be seen the two women and the bodyguards.

"I see 'am. What the hell're they luggin'?"

Bobbie Lee squinted. "Picnic basket, looks to me. Uh-huh, a picnic basket, right there. Lord, they're gonna have a picnic. Life's like that, ain't it, full of bad guys a-havin' fun?"

"They're s'posed to be birders, not beach fuckers. Guessin' they've got cheese and woine too. ... T'is es really seck."

Bobbie Lee balled up a fist, her eyes on the party as they ambled toward the beach. "Well, let 'im come. Let's jist keep walkin' and go back to the car. Then we'll come back ... an' see how they're doin'."

Once inside the SUV, they opened a bottle of spring water and looked again at the map of the beach and grounds.

"Wish this was sour mash," said Bobbie Lee, wrinkling her nose.

"T'is es batter for you. Everyt'ing's about health now."

"How do *you* know?"

"Cause et's at the beach. Everbody knows t'at. You're only s'posed to drenk water at the beach, et's batter for your sken."

"What's that, another cholesterol thing? About every two weeks they've gotta come up with somethin' like that. This is good for you, that's bad for you, and every goddamn vegetable you eat's gonna build your bones and cure your cancer. It's all a bunch of lies. They come up with that stuff because they're bored. I still wish there was Jack in this here bottle."

Connors tipped the bottle up, then swallowed slowly. "But there esn't," she replied.

"I know that, I jist now said that. How could I wish there was, if there already was, girl?"

"Ever have Irish coffee?"

Making a face, "No. When I first heard 'bout it, it sounded so revoltin' that I never wanted to try it."

"Prob'ly would be here, but en Ireland et's good."

"Think I should move to Irelan'?"

"There's prob'ly a couple t'ings you wouldn't loike, ef you ded."

"Yep, I can see that. ... So, are you sure you don't wanna call Kissler?"

"No."

"You're not sure?"

"No, I mean I don't want to call 'em."

"Well, we are killin' four people instead of one, which is somethin' he might like to know about."

"I'm not really a moralist. I don't give a fuck what he moight loike to know about. We've been over t'at."

Bobbie Lee put her head back and sighed. "I know. And I agree with you. Jist checkin', girl."

"We'll talk to Martina when we gat back. But she's savvy about Kassler, too."

"I'm jist wonderin' who else would be with us, exactly. This ain't no baby step."

"Martina, Stanley, and Maggie. I would assume Gratchan sees roight t'rough the bastard. I'm not worried about Packard, he'd kell Kassler joost to kell 'em."

"I figgered that. Which leaves Bradley. Good ole Brad. He could go either way. That boy could sell us out in a heartbeat, *all* of us, turn his back on the whole shithouse, jist like that. And they'd drape him in medals for doin' it."

"I'd be glad to shoot the fucker."

Bobbie Lee looked at her, handing her the bottle. "Sure, if it comes to it, that'd be great."

"No, I mean now. That way, we wouldn't have to worry about et."

With another look, "Well, he's jist one prick. But with the rest of this deal, you are talkin' treason, you know that, right? I mean, let's jist say it out loud right here in the car, so it's out there, right on the tabletop—treason. You're ready for that?"

"Are you?"

"Well, yeah, but I'm from Tinnessee."

"And I'm from Cork."

"So, yeah. So, maybe they'll jist kill us. ... That'd be a whole lot better'n dyin' in some goddamn Union prison, please." When there was no response to this, she said, "Come on, let's change the subject and talk about somethin' happier. We've got work to do. Let's go find these here picnickers and see if they're enjoyin' their lunch."

At the dunes, they chose the shorter path to the beach and made their way to the top of the gravel-and-sand embankment. Unable to see the woman or her companions, they set out across the lengthy stretch of sand toward the ocean. Finally rounding the northern end of the old military installation, they saw them sprawled out upon their blanket and sipping at champaign glasses. Only a few other blankets spotted the seascape, and one man, a hundred yards or so away, splashed ankle-deep along the surf with a dog.

"They haven't seen us," said Connors. "Et's pairfect. Whan we gat close you ask 'am somet'in' about birds. Shoot the guard closest to you, and I'll take the other one. Same with the women. Aye?"

"Got it. Let's go. Sling your camera in front. Let's go."

They talked and chatted as they made their way toward the party. At about thirty feet away, they saw one of the guards stop his conversation and begin to eye them. At twenty feet, his face went rigid. At ten, Bobbie Lee delivered her query, moving to her right as Connors moved left.

"Hey," said Bobbie Lee as they were now upon them, "we're lookin' for families of gulls. Seen any?"

As one of the men put his glass down and started to get up she pulled the 9mm from her back pocket, stuck it in his face and fired. As the blast knocked him back down Connors pulled her shirt up, yanked the .38, and shot the second man twice, first in the chest, then in the head. Instantly the target's companion let out a wretched scream, which was silenced when Bobbie Lee shot her in the mouth, then in the neck. The target herself, still holding her champagne, as if about to take another sip, simply stared, but only for a moment, for Connors put her gun to the woman's temple and fired. Then quickly they put another bullet into each victim's head and walked away, holstering as they walked.

Reaching the dunes, they climbed the path again, then turned to look for the man walking the dog. He had stopped and was staring at them from the edge of the surf. The other parties, much farther away, had not seemed to notice.

For a moment Connors watched as the dog played in the shallow water around the man. Then she muttered, "Poor dog."

Inside the SUV, Bobbie Lee started the engine, then pulled the shift into reverse. "Well, I guess we won't be enjoying this pritty scenery for awhile. But it was nice."

At the highway, they turned toward Cape May. As they drove through the town, past the antique dealers, past the Acme, past the Wawa, they chatted. Crossing the little bridge, they could just see the white sail of a fairy-tale yacht as it slipped away from the harbor.

At the summit of Cape May's main bridge Connors opened her phone. "Yeah," she said simply. "Et's done. We're out. . . . Yeah, headin' back now. . . . No, four. . . . Yeah. . . . Yeah, the girlfriend and a couple of bodyguards—who, by the way, looked loike fuckin' pros. . . . Yeah, that's roight. . . . We got 'em on the beach. . . . Roight. . . . Yeah, talk to you later. . . . Bye."

Bobbie Lee shifted her hands on the wheel. "What'd he say?"

"The fucker was all nonchalant about et."

"He's a dick."

"Aye."

Adjusting her sunglasses, "Know somethin'? I'm gonna miss that Lucky Bones place. They've got some people in there what can cook, and that's a fact. I ain't never cooked like that in my life. And eatin' on the docks at that other place, with them little boats honkin' their horns and all, and with them seagulls flyin' around, that was practic'ly idyllic. We jist gotta go back there someday."

"The Lobster House."

"Yeah, that was it, that's right."

"I loiked t'at, too. We'll have to go back, try somet'in' alse."

"Yeah, they had a lot on that menu. My mouth's a-waterin' right now, girl."

"So, what can you say you learned about birds?"

"Didn't git a chance to learn nothin', there was too much shootin' goin' on, had to keep my head down. But I like birds. They're real beautiful, and they represint a lot of things, like liberty and everything. What do you think?"

Connors looked at her, then queried, "Want to be a birder, gat the scope and all the stuff?"

"Prob'ly not. Wouldn't have the time—I'm too busy fightin'. Hey, what say let's stop somewhere and git somethin' to eat?"

"Sure. We could order some seafood."

"Not for me, thanks. I had a real good time back there and don't want to spoil my memories. Think I'll jist git a hamburger and a soda pop. Yeah, I'm gonna miss Cape May. But we'll go back someday. Might should give it some time, though."

"Maybe a lettle."

CHAPTER 11

Lancaster County, Autumn

The Osipovs returned from Italy to find Maggie and Packard nearly in love. Or at least, that was how Martina put it, referring to the glow she claimed to see on Maggie's face. Unoffended, Maggie merely shrugged and smiled, but in fact the difference in her behavior toward the man could not be denied. She now called him Lenny instead of Mr. Packard and swore she had developed a fondness for the blended aromas of Hoppe's and Jack Daniel's. If she admitted, albeit secretly to Martina, that his grumpiness was probably perpetual, she at once insisted that his character was replete with admirable qualities. Stanley, for his part, found it all charming and said that nothing should hinder their romantic plans, whatever they might be. It would be immoral, he declared, to impede such a union, since obviously their stars had aligned.

"What do you care for the stars?" demanded Martina, her brow raised. "You do not watch the stars."

"I watch many things," he returned facetiously.

"You watch me disrobe," she teased back. "And now you are an astrologer and can state that two people's stars have aligned?"

But after turning the light out and kissing her breasts, he replied that anybody could see that nature, whether that included the stars or not, was in agreement with both his and her assessment that Maggie and Packard were in love. Therefore they should be encouraged.

The real post-vacation color, however, was provided when Gretchin and Bradley returned from Atlantic City. She claimed that he had spent an entire evening plying her with martinis as they gambled at the blackjack tables and then later in their room had practically raped her. In answer to this accusation, he simply remarked that she had only turned out to be the slut he had always suspected her of being. To the obvious reaction of Martina at the singularity of the word *room*, they both replied that a casino booking error had left them no choice but to share the same room.

Neither Connors nor Bobbie Lee cared to take the vacation that Kessler had suggested. Instead, they filled the autumn days with walks together through the fallen leaves of the Estate's trees and with day trips into the Amish countryside on Bobbie Lee's newly acquired Harley Sportster.

She had purchased the motorcycle from a local farmer whose son had walked away from it five years earlier following a near collision with a train.

She then had it reconditioned and painted white at a specialty shop in Lancaster, adding a comfortable rear seat, hinged footrests, and hard saddle bags for gear and small weapons.

It was common for them to ride out for two or three days at a time. But as the weather had grown colder, even the casual jaunt forced them to bundle up and ride extra close to keep warm against the adversary. From the Green Dragon flea market they bought fleece-lined bomber jackets, hand-tooled cowboy boots, and leather riding gloves. Their solidarity in meeting the challenge of the open road became nearly mystical, as they refused, as one, to surrender to the dangers of the highway or the fierceness of the cold. They would roll up to a roadside café for dinner, stop for the night at a country motel, and in the morning wrap up against the cold and again head out onto the open highway. They would ride past farms and watch as Amish children tended their cows. They would pass horse-drawn buggies slowly, waving to the families, but would blow past the big trucks with frenetic speed and the famous blatting Harley roar. And when they stopped during the day, they would eat sandwiches and drink whiskey and reminisce over the Texas rescue, recalling the smooth speed of the Bonneville and the ferocious power of the magnum.

A few days before Thanksgiving, Kessler arrived in the gray sedan. As he and a sidekick agent took seats in the living room of the Big House Bobbie Lee and Maggie rolled in the tea cart, heaped with sumptuous sandwiches and pretty cakes.

"Well," he announced with satisfaction, "I'm so happy with the performance on the Cape May project, I can't put it into words. Just one heck of a job, Kelly, Bobbie, that's all I can say. On behalf of the Agency, I congratulate you. Good work, both of you." Although he failed to catch the eye contact between Connors and Martina that followed this statement, he did pick up on the general silence of the team. Finally he cleared his throat and spoke again. "Uh-hm, I was glad you were able to take care of the bodyguards." And raising a hand to preclude their response, "I'm sorry, we just didn't know about them. Too much info, not enough info—ha. But great work, great work from you guys."

Connors swallowed the tea she had slurped. "But yous sure as fuck knew about the chick, dedn't yous? Yous knew about the chick, but dedn't know about the bodyguards—I moight fuckin' believe t'at."

After staring at her for a moment, then giving the sidekick a pained look, he replied, "God, Kelly, you've always got that raucous mouth, don't you?" When she did not respond, he continued, "We simply didn't know. I'm sorry, I'm really sorry. At least, I'm glad you weren't hurt, either of you."

With a twitch of her nose, "Nah, we wouldn't want t'at to happen."

He shifted his cup to the other hand, then said, "It comes with the job, Kelly. I think you know that."

"What does?" she returned, her tone menacing. "Gattin' hurt, or gattin' bad intel?"

He hesitated. "Both actually. You're not the first agent to receive faulty intel and you won't be the first to get hurt, if that happens, which I sincerely hope doesn't. Bobbie here isn't complaining, are you, Ms. Henry?"

"No," replied Bobbie Lee, "I guess I'm not. But them there guards, with their cut hair and their pieces bulgin', stood out like two goddamn battleships in a river. Even stupid intel couldn't have missed 'em. But yours did."

Now he stared at her too. "Well, we did miss them. We did, and I'm sorry. Now that's all I've got to say about it. If you ladies," and looking around at them, "or anybody else, if you're not happy, you can go ahead and let me know and I'll forward it to the Agency.. Because they want to know. A lot of funding was appropriated for all this—this place here, its amenities—funding that other units would love to have. The economy is very bad, as you know. If you're not happy, the Agency isn't happy, okay? So, I appreciate it when you let me know about things like this, so we can discern your level of contentment." Then he sat back to wait for their response. Suppressing the urge to swallow, he cleared his throat and simply looked around at them.

Bradley, who had been tugging at his shoestring, leaned forward and offered earnestly, "Actually, Paul, I'm very happy. I wasn't aware that the girls here were upset. Intel is never perfect, Kelly, you can't expect it to be, let's face it. I mean, look at how we went into Iraq because of bad intel. We're all adults here, we're savvy. I think the Agency's doing what it can."

Gretchin, as if she had been waiting for the moment, said, "Oh, now bottlehead has spoken, isn't that great. You know, Bradley, bottlehead, if you had any sense you'd realize he just manipulated you."

"Oh good grief!" he returned, shaking his head. "You're pathological, do you know that? Whatever I say, you make me out to be an idiot. So, just shut your mouth, would you?"

"Don't tell me to shut up, mister. You're siding with the wrong people here. In fact, you always do. Every time the Agency pulls its dick out, you suck it."

"Oh yeah? Well, I'll tell you something, slut, I hate you! Now just shut up, would you?"

"No way, prick!"

Kessler, who had to some extent grown accustomed to the crudity of these exchanges, nevertheless felt himself redden. Sometimes he hated not just these two, but all of them. In the beginning, when he was forwarding his theory and pushing for the funding, he had practically gloried in their outspoken manner and crude quarreling. But he had grown weary of their silly expressions of disrespect for each other, their persistent efforts to slander each other, and their disrespect for him too, at least from Gretchin, but also now Connors, of all people, and even the backwater Henry girl.

"Please," put in Maggie, "Gretchin, Bradley, please stop."

But despite the appeal for calm, Bradley pointed his finger at Gretchin and lashed out, "Don't even try to talk out loud, Gretchin, you don't know anything. Just shut up, you're an embarrassment, an absolute embarrassment."

Her eyes narrowed. "Know what, Bradley? It's too bad they don't make condoms to fit your head, because I'm voting for you to get dickhead of the year."

"Shut up, Gretchin, you damned bitch, just shut up!"

"Go back to playing with your goddamn shoe-string." And here she gave him the finger and a quick roll of the eyes.

Finally Martina said, "I think what you're saying, Paul, is that you're going to try to get us better intelligence reports, right?"

Kessler brightened. "Yes, absolutely yes, Martina, yes, thanks, nicely said. Yes, we'll try to do that, get you folks a more complete picture of things, okay? Okay, Kelly, Bobbie?"

While Bobbie Lee sat unresponsive, Connors shifted in her chair, ground her teeth, and began to slurp again at her tea. Bradley, lowering his head, began again to tug at his shoestring.

"Now, if we can," Kessler said genially, "I'd like to move on. I would like to present the next project, if I may. Do you think that's all right, do you? Well, I think it is, too, so that's what I'm going to do."

"Uh-hm," interjected Packard gruffly. "I have a proposal."

Kessler shot the silent agent another look, then calmly said to Packard, "Sure, Len, speak up, what's on your mind?"

As a Doberman might rip at its hide to answer an itch, the grisly Packard took his time at thoroughly scratching the stubble on his chin. His thoughts collected, he then sighed and said, "Maggie and I . . . are serious about each other."

It would have been impossible for anyone in the room to overestimate the difficulty with which the man had said this. Immediately Maggie's eyes began to shine with happiness. Martina, watching her, gave Stanley a pleasant nudge. Gretchin seemed shocked, while Bradley only sat grinning. Bobbie Lee squinted with suspicion as she looked at Packard, then at Maggie, then at Packard again. Connors, apparently indifferent, reached for more tea. Kessler, who had hired the man, the notorious Leonard Packard, because of his reputation as an efficient, emotionless killer, simply closed his eyes in unbelief. What he did not believe was that anyone with so much blood on his hands could ever really come to love anyone at all. He tried to imagine the man laying aside his two Smith & Wessons and kissing Maggie, or God forbid, climbing on top of her, making love to her, and even worse, Maggie letting him do it. But the image seemed to short out in his mind.

"Well," said Kessler, giving his eyelids a quick massage, "well, Len that's . . . quite . . . the news. . . . Sure, well, yes, congratulations. Congratulations to you both. I'm happy for both of you. Yes, uh-huh, great, good. Well, there it is, out on the table. Great, yeah."

"My proposal," rasped Packard, new confidence in his voice, "is for Maggie to take over here at the Estate and have Bobbie Lee come out in the field. Maggie says she's willing, and I'd be happier with her here."

Kessler, the romance images still playing with his mind, queried gently, "Maggie, how about it? What are your thoughts?"

For the first time in years, it seemed, Maggie felt herself blush. "Yes, we are serious about each other, and yes, I think it would be good for me to stay more around here. I'm not really the weapons expert that I should be, anyway, I mean, to give the help I should be giving on the projects. I would be more useful, I think, here at the Estate."

"So, you want to? It's really what you want, yourself?"

"Yes."

"And you won't worry too much?"

Momentarily, her eyes dropping, "Yes, I will, very much."

He sighed, turning toward Bobbie Lee. "And how about you? Ready to go out in the field full time? I know you're a pro, but this isn't what you bargained for."

"You won't have to talk me into it," was the bright reply. "I'm for it, ready to rock 'n roll. Maggie's a better cook than me anyway. I can cook a little, but she's a chef. It'd be an honor to have her here. And the dogs jist love her to pieces. And I'm real happy for her and Len, they're great people. All the best to both of you."

"Okay, I guess that works. We'll keep Maggie's pay at the same level and raise yours to full pay for a field agent. How's that? . . . I would really like to move on now, if we can and talk about the next project. Unless, of course, someone else has an issue to discuss."

Osipov, stretching his legs and displaying the cowboy boots, said, "I have an issue to be raised. You mentioned at the beginning putting in a gun range here. When will that be?"

Kessler looked at him for a moment. How had this man gotten into his life? Yes, he had wanted him on the team for its startup, but instead of getting himself shot, as expected, he had survived to this very moment, and on a full agent's pay, and now sat asking this stupid question. How could his own filthy, dirty Russian people have sent him away, allowed him to live? How?

Osipov returned the look. "Well?"

Unable to conceal his wince at the question, Kessler, his eyes upon the blue boots, replied, "You're right, Stanley, and I'm glad you've brought that up. Actually the paperwork for the facility is on my desk as we speak. I only need to sign it and submit it, which I will do. Okay?"

But the Russian persisted. "What will they go for, can you tell us this, please?"

"Actually I'm not sure. Probably . . . a modest structure. Maybe something a little larger than, say, a garage." Momentarily he added, "There'll be a fan, of course."

"An OSHA-approved fan, is that correct?"

No longer able to control his emotions, Kessler sat forward. "Yes, damn it, a fan, a goddamn fan, okay? An OSHA-approved fan, okay? You won't breathe a thing, not a goddamn thing, okay?"

Martina scratched her cheek. "A fan?"

He looked at her, his eyes bulging. "Yes, a fan, Martina, an exhaust fan. Your husband here wants a fan, so of course we'll put one in. Everything according to Hoyle. Is that good enough?"

"That sounds elaborate, Paul," she replied.

He swallowed, then sat back again. "Well, no, it won't be a terribly elaborate facility, there just isn't the money for that. But I'm pretty sure it'll go through, so don't worry. I'll sign the papers as soon as I get back."

"Are you saying it to us," queried the Russian, "that we will have it by the springtime?"

Faltering, "Yes, well, I should think that might be possible, yes. I'll see what I can do. No promises, of course. You know how bureaucracies can be."

The Russian smiled. "Do I?"

"Well, I'm sure the KGB didn't provide you with gunranges and exhaust fans, Stanley."

"I was not in KGB, you know this."

Now it was Kessler who smiled. "Yes," he replied, "yes, I do."

"Then why did you say it? First, you play with us in the field, now you are playing with us in the house."

When Kessler glared at him, Martina put in, "Why can't we just practice here on the grounds? This is pretty removed out here, what would be wrong with it? Who's to care?"

Kessler turned to her, then nearly whimpered, "I don't see anything wrong with that actually. Maybe that's a good idea."

"And then," she continued happily, "no paper-work, no facility. Just like that. Yes?"

"Sure, yes, I think so," he stammered, with a roll of his eyes. "That would be okay, I think. And there is a recession, of course, so the Agency will be relieved. There isn't a lot of money to spread around."

"We are understanding this," said the Russian. "But then, how is it that you can afford to have the new projects?"

Almost cringing, "What?"

Then Gretchin offered, "You can only afford them if you don't expect to have to pay for any long-term care insurance for us, right?"

"This is correct," put in Stanley. "If the Agency eliminates us by sending us into the more and the more dangerous situations, there will not be any of us left to retire."

"Not *the more and the more*," said Martina impatiently, "just say *increasingly*."

Kessler gulped, and his tone became pleading. "Listen, uh, everyone. I only want to assure all of you that your safety is our priority. We only want your safety, absolutely. Believe me, please. You are all very valuable to us, to your country, in fact."

Adding an extra dose of sugar to her voice, Maggie queried, "Would you like another little cake, Paul? More tea?"

Nearly choking, he replied helplessly, "Yes, uh, Maggie, thank you, I would. I'll have more, yes, thanks."

"So," said Bobbie Lee, with a chuckle, "we can jist go out in the back yard here and fire away. Killy's M-42's a little hot, but we can stick to handguns, I guess. That'll be great, almost as good as Tinnessee."

He smiled, but with pain on his face. "Would it be possible for us to move on now? Is that all right with everyone?"

Gretchin smirked aloud. "Sure. Let's talk about murder, why the hell not? Not that the Agency can afford it, since it's a bureaucracy caught in a recession and strapped for cash. But yeah, that sound's great, let's do that, let's move on and hear about the new project."

He felt his shoulders fall and considered that he might be approaching exhaustion. Excusing himself, he left for the bathroom. When he returned, his eyes red, he sat down and took a small piece of cake and nibbled at it.

"Everything all right, Paul?" queried Martina.

But the meeting was not to continue that day. Feeling drained, Kessler suddenly proposed that his presentation of the new project be postponed until the spring. Before finishing either his cake or his tea, he stood, requested his coat, and then quietly left, with the sidekick following close behind.

CHAPTER 12

The winter months passed uneventful, except for the marriage of Maggie and Packard. There could be no public ceremony, of course, and a justice of the peace was secured. The team's private celebration party would be the only overt expression of the marriage. Kessler turned down his invitation to attend, but had a small, two-slice toaster sent from an online retailer.

But if Maggie experienced any disappointment at not having a normal wedding, Packard clearly did not, muttering crustily that going through such an ordeal would have made his skin crawl. Martina, however, resented not being able to give Maggie away.

Packard then moved into Maggie's room at the Big House, intending to keep his room at the Den as a private space and where he might work with his guns.

"She says she likes the smell of gun oil," he remarked to Bradley, "but the way she puts together a tea tray makes me doubt it."

"Women say a lot of things," returned the other.

"So do men. Everybody does. We all say stuff."

With a grin of curiosity, "That's a little sensitive for you, ain't it, pal? Keep thinking like that and pretty soon you won't be able to pull a trigger anymore. You might work yourself out of a job, have to start gardening or something."

"Yeah," Packard snorted, "and then what would they do, send Kessler out to pull the trigger himself?"

"That's a joke. I don't read him that way. He's too much of a theory guy."

Even during the coldest months Connors and Bobbie Lee continued to go out on the motorcycle. Weekend trips were a favorite. But the winter of the Pennsylvania Dutch country proved formidable, and the bomber jackets and cowboy boots were replaced with full cold-weather riding suits and gear. If forced to wait for the clearing and salting of snowy roads, they would simply grab beers, unfold the map, and plan a future trip. Then they would load the bike and head out into the frigid countryside.

On a bitter Saturday in March, when they had stopped for sandwiches and beer, Bobbie Lee queried, "What do they do in Irelan' for fun?"

"They drenk," replied Connors, removing the toothpicks from her sandwich, "they drenk and screw. How 'bout en Tannessee?"

"About the same. They play with their guns, that's a favorite. They shoot things around the yard, like cans and bottles, and maybe put more holes in the garage door, then maybe drive out and shoot a road sign or two. It's like min'ature golf, it's somethin' to do. And they love cars and trucks and stuff. At night ever'body eats pie and watches TV. They like sports too, and all the kids trade baseball cards. Don't the Irish do that?"

Following a swig of beer, "I don't know much about what the keds do."

Momentarily, "Did you ever play with dolls? . . . You did have dolls, right?"

"Hell fuckin' no."

Bobbie Lee looked at her. "Not even one doll?"

"No."

With a shrug, "Nothin' wrong with that."

"Glad you feel t'at way. I was gonna pea me seat."

"But did you ever want one?"

"Maybe a lettle."

Removing a piece of fatty bacon from her sandwich, Bobbie Lee looked across at the colorless eyes, the full lips, the blond hair scrufty from the head gear, the symmetrical shoulders. She had not met many women with as much natural beauty, certainly not combined with as much courage.

"You should git one sometime," she said, "jist fer the hell of it."

"What, for Mary's sake, would I do weth a doll?"

"I don't know, girl. Jist have it around, I guess. Set it on yer dresser and look at it, I don't know."

"I had a dog."

"Boyfriends?"

"One or two."

"I had one of them in high school—a real mean bastard. The guy was always tryin' to git his finger wet. He jist wouldn't leave me alone."

"They're all loike t'at."

Bobbie Lee looked down at her sandwich. "I like bacon, but look at this stuff—all fat."

"Don't eat et."

"I'm hungry, it's either eat this'n or order another'n. Then I'll git fat, 'cause I've already eaten half of this'n."

"You're too skenny to gat fat. Your muscles bulge loike rocks."

Bobbie Lee closed the sandwich after extracting another piece of the bacon. "You know somethin'? If I had your looks, I'd sell 'em for a house and a swimmin' pool."

"Horseshet, you're pretty as a pecture."

"Well . . . I did have a hillbilly tell me I had nice tits. Now I can't find 'em."

"Hellbellies?"

"No—tits. Matter of fact, when he said that, I went right home, pulled my shirt off, and looked in the mirror—no tits. And the same now, at least none to speak of."

"He loiked you?"

"No, he was lyin'. I jist sent him on his way, and no sugar. But I'll tell you what, you've got the physique stuff."

"You've got some of et yoursalf."

"Naw, downright homely compared to you. Tits, ass, you got it all, sweetheart. You come outta the shower and walk across the room in your birthday suit—whoa. Yeah, if I had stuff like that, I'd pick me out a banker, that's right."

"I'm gattin' flabby."

Bobbie Lee set her beer down. "No, that ain't flabb. But I'll tellya what, we'd better git you in a car, 'cause ridin' a motorcycle'll give you ass warp. And then where'll you be? No house and no swimmin' pool."

"No banker."

"Yeah, you're a real piece of tail, sweetheart, as they say in the South."

"What part of the South?"

"Oh, pritty much all over."

Connors put her beer down. "Esn't et funny? An Irish man would sell his soul for a girl loike you, with t'ose lettle tets and long brown hair, but all you want to do es roide around on a Hairley and kell people."

With a sigh, "You're sure gittin' to be philosophical, girl."

"Joost observin', t'at's all."

"Uh-huh. Well, while you're observin', you might want to make a note—my hair ain't brown, it's chestnut. ... I natur'ly love motorcycles and guns, but I got kinda grandfathered into killin' people."

"Sounds rationalistic."

"Jist practical, that's all."

Connors looked into the sulfur-colored eyes and for a moment said nothing. Then, "How'd you gat t'ose yellow eyes?"

"Drinkin' Jack Daniel's and breathin' motorcycle fumes."

"No, I mean the iris. Wolves have eyes loike t'at."

Bobbie Lee looked into her empty bottle. "So, maybe I'm a goddamn wolf."

Later they took a room at a roadside inn, and as they lay in the dark of the tiny space Connors queried softly, "What ded your family want you to be?"

"Good question. They never really said. I think they jist wanted me to be happy. My mom prob'ly wanted me to git married and drop a bunch of kids. . . . How 'bout you?"

Clutching her .38 under the covers, "Me ma wanted me to be a nun, I'm pretty sure. She brought et up en her own ways. She dedn't push et, but I'm pretty sure."

Bobbie Lee slid a hand under her pillow and reposition the P-64. "Is that why you have that rosary?"

"No, I have et for mesalf. I say et sometoimes."

"To Mary?"

"T'at's who you say et to. You've gotta gat your nose out of your Bible and learn somet'ing."

Momentarily, "Do you think she minds the blood on your fingers when you count them beads?"

"Prob'ly."

One evening following dinner, after Connors and Bobbie Lee had returned from a weekend ride, Martina buttoned her sweater, stood up, cleared her throat, and addressed the team, "As team leader, I want to talk to everyone about the next project. I don't know what it is, but I'm sure we'll soon be hearing from Paul."

Putting his cup down, Bradley queried, "What's to talk about?"

Stanley eyed him for a second, but said nothing.

"Well," replied Martina, "not a whole lot really. But I think we should just all keep our eyes open as to the circumstances—I mean, during the project."

Bradley leaned forward. "Meaning what? We always keep our eyes open, right? I mean, it goes along with the territory, right? So, what are you getting at, Martina?"

Averting her gaze, "I think we should always be cautious when assessing the situation we find ourselves in."

"But you don't need to say that," he returned. "What are you talking about? You're getting at something else."

"I just want everyone to be safe."

"Again," he said, "not necessary to say."

"All we need to do," she continued, as if he had not spoken, "is to be aware of any disparity."

He frowned. "Disparity?"

Gretchin, straightening her back, put in, "Yes, Bradley, a word you can't spell, let alone define."

Ignoring this, he said to Martina, "Could you be clearer?"

With a sigh, she replied, "Yes. We need to look out for ... actually we need to expect that the projects will turn out to be different from what the Agency has described."

He frowned again. "Different? How?"

She looked at him. "More dangerous—much more dangerous."

"When you say the Agency, you mean Paul. I know that's what you're saying."

Gretchin slammed her fork down. "Jesus, Bradley! What is fucking wrong with you? Yes, she means Paul. Or maybe not just Paul, maybe the whole Agency, what's the difference?"

"Here we go again," he moaned. "It's not just faulty intel now, is it? It's intentional, right? It's a plot. Really? Boy, do I know you people, or what?"

Scowling, "She just wants us to be prepared."

"I don't want to hear it."

"And if things get worse? You know, not just two bodyguards they didn't tell us about, but four or five or maybe a whole fucking army of them?"

He chuckled. "Yeah, that's what I thought. I know you people, you're intent on proving that they're trying to get rid of us, or at least that Paul is."

She leaned forward. "He considers his theory proven."

"I know, I know—he doesn't need us anymore, right? Boy, you people are paranoid."

"You don't even consider it to be possible?"

"Why do you care what I consider, Gretchin?"

"Because, dope, I usually ride with you, and I need you to cover my ass."

He pursed his lips. "Well, everybody here knows what I think. It's preposterous. Nobody's trying to get us killed, and that's all I have to say about it." And turning to Martina, "Paul's a good guy, he picked us, we're his team. You people insinuate a lot. I knew what you were getting at when he was here, and you know where I stand about the Agency *and* Paul."

"Yes," said Gretchin, "we do, Bradley. How could we miss it, asshole, since you practically suck the man's dick every time he's here. You do, you ingratiate yourself all over the place. God! Half the time, I expect you to salute him."

"Stick to the facts."

"And what would you do with the facts, process them?"

"I'm too stupid, right, Gretchin? You know, after you people finish talking, I always still believe in the Agency. They just don't operate that way. They don't use you and then get rid of you. They're Americans, and Americans don't operate that way."

"Anybody," she said, "who falls for so much shit, is full of shit himself. No, you're not just stupid, you're worse. What about the bodyguards, bub? You're telling us he didn't know about the bodyguards, the professional bodyguards? He knew about her hobby, her girlfriend, all of it, but not the bodyguards? Just bad intel, right? Sure."

Osipov then offered, "KGB was very stupid sometimes, too. But when things were *too* stupid, it could not be missed that somebody was making a conspiracy."

At this, Bradley simply shrugged and then picked up his cup again.

That night, when Connors went up to bed, she found on her pillow a pretty blond doll clothed in a frilly dress and wearing patent leather shoes. A note, propped against the pillow, read *A little gift from Tennessee.*

For a moment, she felt nothing, as if stunned by the fall after being shot. Then she closed her eyes and began to cry softly.

It was three days later that Kessler called Martina to tell her about the project and to say that he could not come to visit as usual. She was to relay the information he would give her to the team and expect a fuller explanation by special mail.

Closing her phone, she said to Maggie, "This bastard's pretty crazy."

"What did he say?"

"It wasn't what he said, but how he said it. There's just something funny about the guy, and it's getting funnier all the time. I'm thinking it's my paranoia talking, but somehow my eyes seem to be opening more and more every time I talk to him."

During dinner she opened her notepad, perused her script, then spoke. "I just wanted to let you all know that Paul called today. We have a new project."

"See there," Bradley said, tapping the table with a finger, "right on time. He's reliable."

Gretchin gave her head a shake, and smiling at him, said with contempt, "Wow, Bradley. Wow. You need a trainer."

"Paranoia's a cruel master, people," he returned, "take my word for it."

Continuing, Martina relayed the information concerning the project. The targets were two men who had attempted but failed to bomb a bus in Tel

Aviv in 2010, then fled undetected to the U.S. Through a detailed tip the FBI identified the men as working at a vineyard in New York state. The vineyard owner had temporarily hired them to help with work through the winter months and into the spring. She became increasingly suspicious of their character, however, until one of them inadvertently exposed a gun while loading boxes of wine. Instead of contacting the police, she called the FBI, who in turn called Interpol, who finally called the CIA.

"That it?" grunted Packard?

"We'll get photos," she said, "when the packet arrives, but from what Paul says, it's all dead on. Now it's up to us to put them down. Everybody has been looking for these guys, and now we've got them. But the real issue is time, they were only hired until the spring, so basically we have to go—now."

"A gun?" queried Gretchin. "Which means what, an arsenal? And not just two men, but a bunch of them?"

With a sigh, "Possibly."

But Stanley said, "Probably."

Martina gave him a look, then chimed, "Okay, yes, probably."

"What does this mean," he added facitiously, "that as my wife and as the team leader you are agreeing with me?"

Another look, but one which quickly softened. "Yes."

"Wait a minute," put in Bradley. "I protest. I'm against what you're saying, and I want to go on record as saying I'm against it."

Gretchin rolled her eyes. "We don't keep records here, asshole."

Ignoring her and pointing to his heart, he said, "No treason here—get that straight, people."

"Bradley," said Gretchin, squinting at him, "don't try to be literary or you'll look twice the fool."

"No treason here," he insisted, making a defiant face at her.

"You are so stupid," she jeered. "Talk about treason, what about loyalty to us? What about your semper fi to *us,* don't we count? We go into battle with you, fuckhead, we're at your side, we kill people with you. Remember us?"

"Now, hold up," said Martina forcefully, "nobody's talking treason, no body's talking anything yet. Cool off, you two, we don't need that right now."

"Besides that," Gretchin continued hotly, "if we're right about it all, it wouldn't be treason. That's not treason, it's self-defense, it's survival."

Bradley, giving her a dismissive wave, simply muttered, "Dumb."

"Okay," said Martina, "just let it go, right now. We need to get on with this."

But Gretchin came back at her, "It's his fault. Look at him sitting there, it's obvious he's not with us and would never stand up for us. If push came to shove with the Agency, he wouldn't take our part."

Bradley lifted his chin defiantly. "I'm a patriot, Gretchin, a patriot. Is that a concept you just don't know anything about, huh?"

"I know you are, Bradley," she returned. "You're a true American patriot, great. I don't have a problem with that, it takes all kinds, as far as I'm concerned. I'm not saying I'm a patriot like you are, I'm saying that for me survival trumps patriotism, and if this country, even in the form of Kessler, turns on me, I will try to survive against it. I have a feeling, Bradley, you wouldn't try, and you wouldn't try to help me survive, either. Your sense of country trumps your sense of family—you know—*us.*"

Insistently, "He's a good guy."

"But what if he's not, pal? And worse, what if the Agency knows he's not? What if people in the system actually intend to use us and then junk us, what then? Where are you going to stand then? You're going to stand with them, with him, the Agency, the system, them and not us, that's what I'm saying. We're you family, and you won't stand with us. And I rest my fucking case, okay?"

"He's a good guy," he repeated. "He wouldn't do it."

"He's human, and so are they, Bradley. He might do it, he might be doing it as we speak."

"I don't believe he is."

"But he might be. And if he is, you won't be covering my back, will you, Bradley? You'll be covering his."

He leaned back in his chair, hung an arm over its corner, and looked away.

"Okay," said Martina wearily, "now that we've talked it just about to death, let's admit that it might also not be happening. Right now, let's concentrate on the project. This is the job, the work, so let's do it."

CHAPTER 13

At breakfast the next morning Bradley jovially threw out the question, "Tell me something, who's the greatest general in history?"

Bobbie Lee answered, "Robert E. Lee. Who the hell else could there be?"

"Great," he replied happily. "Well, that's an answer. And you could be right too, who knows? Anybody else got an idea?"

"I have a feeling," quipped the Russian wearily, "that you do."

Bradley gave the table a benign slap. "Come on, Osipov, here we are, eating a wonderful breakfast of fried eggs, bacon, zucchini, and coffee, relaxing and with no pressure, and you don't have an answer. I'm amazed. Really, now, what's your answer, hit me with your best guy, come on."

The Russian sighed. "Zhukov."

"Zhukov? Really?"

"Yes."

After a pronounced snicker, "And what about Patton? What would you say about him, comrade?"

"Not bad. A good general really."

"But?"

"He did not play a major role, that is it, no major role."

"Ho! No major role, just like that. He didn't win the war, I suppose?"

"No, and neither did America."

"Oh, good grief."

"America played the role," returned Stanley, "of a third-party player, at best. It was a minor role, important on the chessboard, but not major. It was industrial and symbolic, but it was not major."

"Ho, ho! Unbelievable."

"The sacrifice of the Americans was very small actually. Between three and four hundred thousands, not millions."

"That's because they could fight better. And they were more efficient, that's all." He gave the other a wave of dismissal. "Give me a break. You Russians!"

Maggie gently cleared her throat. "I believe Monty would qualify."

"And Eisenhower wouldn't," protested Bradley. How about it, Osipov? Monty and Eisenhower, what do you think?"

"Even Nikita Khrushchev was better, I am thinking."

Bradley tapped his mug with his spoon, as though counting off the seconds before exploding. "That's disgusting."

"I am being un-American, correct?"

Looking into the pale blue eyes, he answered, "Correct."

"Listen to me, even Rommel was better general than Eisenhower. Eisenhower was already playing president at D-Day. Patton was ten times the general as Eisenhower, and Patton could not polish boots of Zhukov, except of course in American movies."

"That's insulting, that's absolutely insulting. Do you know where you are?"

"I do."

"What about your cowboy boots? You wear cowboy boots because you want to be American, obviously."

Pulling his wire rims down to look over them, "I am hating to be telling you this, mister Sousa, with your horns, your drums and your little flag, but cowboys are really just Texans. And Texans are telling the whole world, including America, to kiss their ass. You should study history just the little bit, and the air would come out of your chest."

"A lot you'd know about it," Bradley shot back. "Russians open a book, and they get sent to the gulags, right?"

A sigh. "Not actually correct. You are being simplistic. Which is joke—when are you not being simplistic? Whole Russian populations did not get sent to gulags. Just a few dissident writers, who ended up here in U.S. Admit it, you are being contemptuous of something you have been told is bad, and you have very little understanding of that thing."

"You make me sick, Osipov. Why don't you just shut up and eat your American breakfast."

"But," put in Maggie, "there was de Gaulle and countless other generals too, and I'm sure they didn't sit around a breakfast table, poking forks at one another."

Bradley held up his hands. "I was just having fun. What's wrong with that? Osipov here has to get all serious."

"You started it, Bradley," said Gretchin.

"I only asked a question, simple as that."

"*Simple* is right."

"Gretchin," he returned, "you should play a different record."

"Record?" she mocked.

Resting a hand on his chest, "You think you're so smart, don't you? You're savvy, huh?"

Closing her eyes, "No, Bradley, forget it, just skip it."

"Oh yeah?" he returned. "How about—GFY. How about that, Gretchin? GFY."

Martina put her cup down sharply. "Okay, okay, I've finished. Good breakfast." And pushing her chair from the table, "Listen, I'll come up with a plan, and we can all talk it over this evening. We'll be going soon."

"Hey," said Bobbie Lee, closing the door behind her as she entered Packard's room, "how's it goin' there? Whoa, I could smell that stuff down the hall."

"The whiskey?"

"No, the cleaner. How's Maggie like that?"

Closing an eye and looking down the barrel of the magnum he had been cleaning, "She says she doesn't mind it, and I believe her—sort of."

Pulling up a chair, "Does love do that?"

"What?"

"Let you believe a lot?" And when he didn't respond, she said, "I wanna talk to you for a second, if you don't mind."

He put the gun down. "Shoot."

"I have a suggestion."

He did not look at her. "I hate people who have suggestions. It's a fault I have, I guess. But yeah, they usually end up offending me."

"Well then," she said with a sigh, "I have the feelin' that I'm just about to make an enemy here. I like Maggie. And I like you, you're a great guy. And I want the best for both of you."

He did not look at her, but picked up the gun and began to wipe it tenderly with an oily rag. "I also hate people who want the best for me," he rasped. "I don't trust them."

"But then, you don't trust anybody."

"Nope."

"I suppose that's good. Neither do I. . . . But listen, I'm gonna say my little thing here. You're both older, and you're obviously in love."

"Meaning what, not much time left?"

"Everybody gets bad cards, Len."

"So?"

"You've both got a lot to lose. Why not consider retiring, both of you, before the project? I think you should consider taking Maggie down to Florida right now, on the spot. Jist resign. Write your letter, leave it on the table, walk out."

He chuckled, showing his yellowed teeth. "I don't think they'd need a letter. They'd just shred it anyway." Flipping out the gun's cylinder, he looked at her. "Why?"

"Not sure."

Now he growled, "What the hell's that mean?"

"Not sure," she repeated. "Maybe I don't wanna hear Martina call Maggie and tell her that some creep out there has jist blown your face off, that the guy she's waited for all her life is gone."

Now his eyes went to hers, and setting the Smith down, he said, "I know what you're saying. I've been thinking about it, too, of course I have. How could I not?" He gave his ear a pull, then ran the oily fingers lightly over the gun's grip. "I'm glad you stopped in, really. She's a wonderful woman, and I'm an old killer. That's all, just a hired killer. You know, I kill people practically for the fun of it. Not for my country or anything like that, but for the exercise of it, because I'm good at it. And then I sleep like a baby at night."

"Well, that might be a little simplistic, Len. You also sleep with a gun in your hand, I'm sure."

"Yeah, you're right. But anyway, Maggie's just so wonderful." He looked at her again. "I'd sell my soul for that woman, you know that?"

"You don't have a soul."

"Yeah," he chuckled, "right again."

"Hell's bells, Len, go to Florida, jist take her and go. I'm sure you've got your scars, but you've been lucky, you're still alive. That's great, but everybody gets bad cards eventually."

"And the project?"

She stood up, walked to the door and pulled it open. "We don't need you, Maggie does."

Gretchin set the glass of ice on her desk, then filled it a quarter full of gin. There was nothing like the smell and taste of Bombay Sapphire on ice for managing the demons. Without the gin, she would have to endure their malicious antics. She tilted the glass to melt more of the crystals. To her, ice formed in a refrigerator's freezer tasted like dead shrimp, but this stuff, that came in a plastic bag, from the store, tasted pure and clean. Having Sapphire over pure ice was like experiencing a little taste of heaven. As she tipped the glass up, then slowly swallowed some of the miraculous liquid, an image of the man in the sports car came to her. The scene had become a demon that must be managed. She shook her head and took another drink. Perhaps someday someone could explain to her just why God ever invented humans in the first place. Fondly she ran a finger along one of the brushes from her studio, a simple tool to create and communicate with, truly one worth inventing. Putting the glass under her nose, she drew a full breath, then took another sip of its contents. Then another image came, not of the man with the hole in his head or of the smoking gun in her hand, but of the students in her art class back at school. Those were good days. She would come home after teaching, make herself a dinner, and then draw until she got sleepy. After a shower, she would go to bed and sleep in peace. Those were good days, peaceful days.

After a knock at the door, she opened it to Maggie, who presented a smile and two cups of chocolate topped with marshmallows.

"Thought you might want one of these," Maggie said, stepping in and setting one of the cups down. "Not much chocolate, extra mild."

"Thanks, great. Here, sit down. I was just slogging some gin."

"Drowning anything?"

"Not really."

"Sure?"

After a sip of the cocoa, "No, I'm not sure."

"There's nothing wrong with drowning stuff—I've got a lot of it that needs doing something with. . . . Do you mind the marshmallows?"

"No, they're good. A few won't hurt."

"So, what were you drowning, if I can ask?"

"What would you guess, Maggie?"

"I don't know, maybe a man in a yellow Austin-Healey. . . . Or how about a certain man in a yellow Corvette?"

"Bradley? You know, I might end up killing that twerp. . . . This is fun, maybe I'll come to your room sometime and put my nose into your life. Shall I bring chocolate?"

Tenderly, "If you do, I'll resent it. Do you resent it?"

"Not entirely, I guess."

A chuckle. "Well, most women seem to be worried about their looks, but I'm not going to guess somebody as pretty as you is drowning her anxiety over that. You're smart, you have great hair, and you've got so much sex appeal that, . . . well, never mind."

"Wow, I was just trying to get a little drunk. Now I have you guessing what I was trying to drown. This is cute."

With a chuckle, "I'll bet you miss the past—the painting, the teaching, the way life used to be with the team."

"Congratulations, Maggie. You've put the hammer right down on the goddamn nail."

"I miss it, too, actually. I can't express how much I miss it. Martina and I had something very special. Just being around her made life very sweet for me. I miss the discussions over tea—just talking with her. I miss hearing her voice. I don't hear it in the same way, you know. When Stanley came along, everything changed."

"Sorry, Maggie. Love breaks things, doesn't it?"

"Before they fell in love, I saw life as a beautiful thing. I had her all to myself. I'm glad that I can still be with her, but it's not the same."

"So, this is stuff you'd like to drown?"

"It is."

"Want some gin?"

"Thanks, but no."

"And how does Len fit into all this?"

"Perfectly, I think. We're perfect for each other. We love each other. Martina found Stanley, and I found Lenny, and everything is what it is, that's all."

Finishing her chocolate, Gretchin set the cup down. "Hey, thanks for being real, Maggie."

Momentarily, "You know, nobody would blame you if you wanted to leave the team, go back, even teach again."

"Well, Bradley would be glad to see me go."

With a chuckle, and scooping up the cups, "I've got to get Lenny packed."

"He lets you touch his guns, huh?"

"Yes, and I let him touch mine."
"Ha, well said."

CHAPTER 14

The Finger Lakes, New York

Listening for the primeval drone as she backed off on the throttle, Bobbie Lee slowed the Sportster, then moved it from the two-lane highway and onto the gravel shoulder. She braked, brought the machine to a halt, and let its hot engine go into idle. With both boots down, she looked up. The sun was bright and the sky very blue, but far away to the north, dark clouds were forming.

"The air's real clear here," she said over her shoulder. "But look out there. That storm's gonna have somethin' to say, I'll bet."

Connors removed her helmet, then got off to stretch her legs and loosen her shoulders. "I hope we gat to the place before t'at storm does."

"Hey, and look at that view. Those're all vineyards, I guess. Ain't that beautiful? That's almost as pritty as Tinnessee, I swear. Maybe I'll move up here sometime. It's sure peaceful, kind of like Maine. Ever bin to Maine?"

"No."

Bobbie Lee pulled her gloves off and laid them across the tank. "Cold as hell up there. I'll bet it's cold here too in the winter. Maybe I shouldn't move here. . . . Well, I'm ready to drink some wine, how 'bout you?"

Declining to answer, the other gave the back of her neck a slow squeeze, then began to walk back and forth beside the guardrail. With her eyes upon the vast landscape, she took deep breaths, exhaling with satisfaction. No place could really compete with Ireland as a source of peace for her soul. But this area east of the Finger Lakes, this land of charming vineyards and famous wines, was beginning to seduce her.

"How 'bout it?" Bobbie Lee asked again.

"What?"

"Are you ready to drink some wine?"

"You're supposed to taste et fairst. Smell et and taste et."

Cheerily, "I've heard that. We might could do that." She gave the throttle a quick turn, then popped her chinstrap free and unsnapped her goggles. "Wonder if there's many bugs around here. Haven't seen a road bug yet. These here goggles still look brand new. How's the ride? We've been goin' for about two hours since that diner. Ass hurt?"

"No, I'm foine."

"You should be, I paid enough for that seat. You could prob'ly sleep on that seat." Then snapping the goggles back in place, "Hey, we should git goin'. Listen to that motor, ain't it pure? There's a lot of cc's in this big boy."

Connors looked down at the massive machine. "Et's good for the road, but maybe a lettle too big for town."

"What're you talkin' about, girl? I could run this here beast right down the middle of a Nashville sidewalk. Don't be bad-mouthin' it, now."

"At least et's not Brettesh."

"What d'ya mean *at least?* This guy's the real deal. Have some respict, girl, this ain't no simple motorsickle, this here's a Harley-Davidson, king of the whole la strada."

"Can't argue weth t'at, et's hauled us here."

"Hell, I ain't even turned it out yet. This boy can run a hundred miles an hour with both of us on his back and not break a sweat. This thing's a goddamn monster. You wait, you may git to see him go. . . . Come on, now, git on, we'd better git goin'. Them clouds're lookin' closer, I think."

Connors pulled her helmet on, then swung a leg over. Tugging on the road gloves, she said, "Et does run noice."

Pulling her gloves home, Bobbie Lee said back to her, "I used to work on 'em a little bit m'self, tune 'em up and all. I was pritty good with a wrinch. I don't play with wrinches anymore, I jist play with guns." And checking her mirror, she let out the clutch and ran them out on to the highway. Bringing them up to speed, she put a thumb up and yelled over her shoulder, "You could prob'ly run moonshine with a Harley!"

Connors responded by slipping her arms around her and giving her a hug. Soon the wind was whipping them with their hair. They could have tucked it into their jackets, but today they let it hang out and fly.

Martina emerged from the motel office just as the motorcycle entered the grounds. When they had pulled up next to the SUV, she said to them, "We're in 6, 8, and 10. A nearby diner, about two miles away, is supposed to be nice. Did you guys have a good ride?"

Bobbie Lee wiped her nose with the back of her gloved hand. "We did. Only stopped four times, which ain't bad at all. Real pleasant trip. Y'all doin' okay?"

"Oh, beautiful trip up, yes, thanks." Eyeing the sleek leather road gear, she added, "I hadn't realized what a strong impression you two make on this—"

"Hairley," said Connors with a grin.

With a chuckle, "I know that, yes, I know that, but I mean, just the whole biker image thing, quite nice really. I've seen you go out from home a few times, but coming in just now, with the leather and everything, well, it's colorful. How fast does this thing go?"

Bobbie Lee wiped her nose again, then wiped the glove clean with the other gloved hand. "Not too fast. Maybe one ten, right now, more if I pump the tires up. But gittin' up there's like ridin' a rocket. This guy can really haul ass."

Blinking, Martina unconsciously pulled the collar of her sweater closer together against the afternoon chill. "Yes, well, very good. I'm sure you can ride the thing."

"Any time you want a ride, Martina, you jist let me know, hear? I'll take you out on the road, show you some speed."

"Perhaps, yes, thanks. Anyway, Bradley and Gretchin have checked in, but are already out to a winery. Can you imagine? Sometimes they seem to get along just fine. So, you two are with Gretchin, in 8, Leonard and Bradley are in 6, and we're here in 10. Come over when you get your things in. Stanley and Len are making coffee. Then we're going for dinner. I'll try to get Gretchin and Bradley to meet us there."

"You would not believe the taste," proclaimed Bradley as the team sat for dinner. He could not refrain from telling them about the uniqueness of the wines he and Gretchin had discovered on their tasting jaunt that afternoon. "The wine around here has a very special something. I can't identify it, but it's great. You've got to try it."

The others did not respond. Instead they looked at Gretchin to either corroborate his findings or not. She said nothing.

Packard, sticking his fork into the pasta on his plate, then offered, "I love spaghetti. There's something special about it, something I can't identify, but it's great."

"Yeah, yeah," Bradley came back. "But wait until tomorrow. You'll see, isn't that right, Gretchin? She said it, too. Go on, tell them, Gretch."

She stared at him. "Who said you could call me that?"

He swallowed. He too had ordered spaghetti. "Who said you could call me Bradley? Or anybody else here, for that matter? You guys just can't get *Brad* out, right? I like *Brad* and I get *Bradley*, you like *Gretchin* and you get *Gretch*. That's fair, right? Right, Gretch?"

"You would like Bud?" queried the Russian. "We could always call you Bud. And Buddy, if we were getting to be knowing you. Or I suppose, even Budley." And giving a little wave, "Hello, Budley."

Bradley sneered at him. "Watch your mouth, Gulag. I don't like Russians. I've got a few names to call you, if I wanted to, you bet."

"I would not be taking that bet," returned Stanley. "It is certain that you have collected a long list of them."

"Oh, it's *Brad,* is it?" said Gretchin. "I've only heard that a thousand times, or maybe ten thousand times. He considers the shorter version to be more manly, more like a football player's name. Anyway, you should all see Brad here taste wine. Nothing special really. It's like watching someone suck up soda at a sports event. It's entertaining, trust me."

Bradley produced a impish grin. "And you're dainty, right? She was just supposed to sniff it, that's what the guy said. But no, she had to snog it, like she was sniffing cocaine. She put on an absolutely wretched show of her ignorance, and now you can trust *me*. How's that, Gretchie baby?"

She pointed her fork at him. "Go buy a pack of rubbers and blow 'em up, idiot, *Bradley*."

Fearing more vulgarity would ensue, Martina put in, "Okay, stop. Decorum, please. We'll all get a chance to see you both in action tomorrow. We're supposed to be here on a tasting tour—wine tasters, sensitive people, here on a tasting tour. Get it?"

Next morning at ten o'clock the proprietor of the Cold Lane Vineyard peeped through the blinds as an SUV rolled to a crunchy stop in the gravel parking lot just in front of her door. She scowled, thinking to herself that another group of tourists were on the prowl. Watching the three get out, especially the gray one, who patted his sport coat ominously, gave her a chill she could not identify. Inherently she did not like people, let alone tourists. Genuine tasters were another grape completely, but why God allowed tourists out of their cities she did not know. When another car pulled in from the opposite direction, a yellow Corvette looking very much also to be from the city, she dropped the blind's blade and rushed to set up the spitting bowl.

Martina entered first, then Stanley, Gretchin, and Bradley. Packard stepped inside last, closed the door, and stood by it, grimly looking around the room. The proprietor watched them for a moment from behind a long counter, then spoke.

"Hi," she offered, obviously making an attempt to be cheery. "Welcome to Cold Lane Vineyard." Then, again clearly deliberately, she put one elbow on the countertop, cocked her head, and said, "What can I show you first?"

"Well," said Martina, moving forward, "we've heard so much about the great wines from this area. I guess we're looking for dinner wines, basically."

The woman lifted her elbow, as if to get to work. "Sure, great. Are you folks from the city? New York?"

"No, Pennsylvania actually."

The woman made her way down the counter, toward the spitting bowl. "We can't sell in Pennsylvania. It's pretty hard to get a license there. You ought to talk to your congressmen or something, get them to open up the state to free enterprise."

"I'm sure they consider they've got that already," replied Martina, lifting a bottle to read its label.

Nearly scowling, the woman shot back, "Well, they don't. We have the best wines in the United States, right here. I can't even ship it there to a private customer. I can ship it to Delaware, but not Pennsylvania or New Jersey. Kind of nuts, I think, and obviously not free enterprise. . . . That's a good red. But why not try this one, it's one of our best blended reds for this season, and it's won a lot of awards, including the Governor's Award."

Pushing a handful of hair behind her ear and taking Bradley's arm, Gretchin queried, "What do you have in whites?"

The woman responded by uncorking two bottles and pushing them across the counter. Then she watched them. She had watched such people do this probably a million times, and now could only anticipate the stupid, pretentious comments they were sure to make.

Bradley snatched up the one closest to him. "So, how much is this one?"

The woman stared at him for moment, then replied, "About fourteen, twelve if you take a box."

"Oh God!" muttered Gretchin, pulling her arm from Bradley's and giving him a look of pure contempt. "Did you really have to ask that? You had to ask the price? Can't you show some sensitivity, even a little?" Then she said to the woman, "Beer—that's right, beer. Beer and football, that's it, that's all there is to life, for him. Oh, and cars."

When the rumblings of a motorcycle came from the parking lot, the woman looked up from her presentation. And as Connors and Bobbie Lee came through the door and strode toward her she muttered, eyeing their full leathers, "God, what next, a biker gang? Where you folks from?"

"Well," answered Bobbie Lee, pulling her gloves off, "I personally ain't from above the Mason-Dixon Line, I can tellya that."

Connors grinned. "I'm from some place I'm not allowed to be from."

"Uh-oh, look out," said the woman, with a roll of her eyes. "Well, step forward and join us. We're trying a few reds and whites. But if your after something else, they're on the board up there, including specials. So, speak up, and I'll get it for you. Don't know where you'll carry it on that motorcycle, though."

"Don't plan to," said Connors, her eyes on the board's scrawled list, "we'll drenk et on the road."

A quick blink. "Right, okay, I'll pretend I didn't hear that."

In the early part of the evening, when the team had returned from dinner and were gathered in No. 10, Stanley uncorked a bottle of blended red and poured it into seven glasses. "Okay," he said, lifting his glass and waiting for the others to follow suit, "this is for tomorrow, but let us be drinking it today."

After the toast, Gretchen said, "We might as well be drinking blood."

Bradley nodded with amusement. "Does that bother you, Gretchin?" And when she only smiled he said, "Why don't you act professional, for once?"

But Stanley, draining his glass, said, "I think she is the quite professional one, she is just being poignant, sensitive."

Bradley chuckled. "Which is something you are not, Osipov. Personally I think she just doesn't like the work."

"We don't need that, Bradley," put in Martina. "What we need is to be one. And right now we need to go over the plan. So let's all go through everything step by step. No screwups, which is why we're going in with everything."

"Well," he replied, "we haven't even seen them. They certainly weren't visible at the vineyard."

But the Russian merely shrugged. "We are not needing to see them, I think. The Agency says they will not be working tomorrow and should probably be at home. I think I would like to go with the intel."

"Ho, for once," burst out Bradley. "Now you believe them."

Another shrug. "Not entirely. But we are not detectives."

"No, but we should be patriots. I'm a patriot."

Gretchin smirked. "All wrapped up, right, Bradley?"

"Why not?" he shot back at her. "The nation state concept is here to stay, and every nation's got a flag, last time I looked. What flag are *you* wearing, Gretchin?"

"I'm not wearing it, dope, that's the point."

"What's wrong with wearing it, if I want to? Osipov here would make his clothes from a Russian flag, I think."

"I don't have a problem with a flag, Bradley," she said, "but I do with simplistic nationalism. God, I do have a problem with that!" And mimicking him, she said, "*I'm a patriot.* God!"

"What's wrong with that? I'm doing this for my country, Gretchin, why is that wrong?"

"Because it defines you."

"And the dragon on your neck doesn't define you?"

She gave the tattoo a scratch.

He put his chin out. "I like doing this job for my country, Gretchin. What are you doing it for?"

With a shake of her head, she replied, "I'm not sure I know, sometimes."

Packard cleared his throat roughly. "I'd like to get to bed, if you folks don't mind. If we're going over things, let's get to it. I'm pretty tired."

"You're right, Len," Martina returned quickly. "All right, step one."

"Great," interrupted Gretchin, gesturing toward Bradley, "I have to ride around with this prick all day and listen to his shit."

Bradley grinned menacingly. "You'll survive."

"Actually," said Martina, "I agree, Gretchin. You always seem to get the better of him."

"Yeah," said Bradley, "because I let her."

Gretchin put both hands up. "And did you have to ask that today, the *price*?"

"Okay, okay," put in Martina, "let it go, it doesn't matter."

"People, please," growled Packard. "I'm an old man, I'm tired, I want to get to bed. If you want to go over this goddamn theater, let's go over it, but please, now, okay?"

CHAPTER 15

Martina moved her fingers over her skin as she considered the corners of her mouth. The grime on the mirror did not help her, she considered, and who would want to check her appearance in such bluish fluorescent lighting? But then, diner restrooms were like that, functional, awful. She did not wear makeup, but perhaps the aging that Maggie had warned her about was beginning to show.

Gretchin, who had been rinsing her hands in the adjacent sink, pulled paper towels and began to dry them. "What're you looking at?"

"The future, or maybe the present."

"I think you've got a few years yet. I wouldn't worry about it."

"Maybe it's time for a little makeup, what do you think?"

After tossing the towel into the basket, "Does your husband say that?"

"No, but that mirror just did."

"Hey, it's the shitty light, don't worry about it. You're still a looker. It's the bone structure and the eyes. If I had stuff like that, I wouldn't need any other equipment. Your looks are magic, trust me. Besides, he loves you."

When they returned to the table Stanley was just putting down the tip, but they sat anyway and took more coffee and chatted. Occasionally Martina let her eyes fall upon the other patrons, the servers, the general movements in the room, and then upon the vast wall mirrors, where it could all be seen again. It was indeed a Saturday like any other, or at least, had become that. The diner itself was like any other diner, a good place to spend any given Saturday, to observe everyday people at their most pleasantly commonplace as they ate and chatted together about everything and yet nothing. She watched as her husband put his wallet away. She lent half an ear as he traded jokes with Packard and Bradley and as Connors and Bobbie Lee discussed plans for a summer camping trip. It would be nice, she mused, if life could be filled with simple chatter, friendly laughter, and benign plans. But it could not. For if life was tender and gentle, it was also harsh and brutal.

Every piece of equipment had been checked and rechecked the previous evening. Stanley's Tokarev rode at the small of his back, and his Makarov, in his waistband. Martina's .38 lay loose in her purse. Packard's magnums rode as usual in the double rig under his sport coat. Connors' M44 carbine, which she had slung, lay on the floor between the SUV's two front seats. In the Corvette

Bradley's 1911 rested in its inside-the-waistband sharkskin, and Gretchin's Glock, in her shoulder purse. Both cars carried enough extra ammunition for a siege. Aboard the Sportster Bobbie Lee carried her Polish P-64 in a friction holster inside the waistband of her jeans, and her Model 19 Combat Magnum, in a shoulder rig inside her road jacket. Connors carried two scandium .38's in a shoulder rig under her jacket.

As the SUV rolled down the two-lane asphalt toward its destination Martina opened her phone and called Gretchin. Momentarily, "Hey. . . . This is it. . . . Yes. . . . Turning in now. . . . Uh-huh. Stay on until we get to the house." Then she turned to look at him. How pleasing his profile was the first time she saw it, and how pleasing it still was!

"They're right behind us," he said, checking the mirror.

In the back seat Packard grumbled to himself as he felt his pocket for the speedloaders. On the Sportster, which brought up the rear of this train, Connors unzipped the front of her jacket, then laid a hand on Bobbie Lee's shoulder.

Near the end of the long dirt driveway, just as the open-porched rancher came into view through the trees, Martina spoke into her phone, "This is it."

When Stanley had brought the SUV to a halt in front of the porch, Bradley parked beside him, about ten feet away and Bobbie Lee pulled the Harley up at the gap, but perpendicular to the other vehicles. All of this was done in a few seconds, and engines were left running. Then Stanley quickly got out, grabbed a box from the back seat and, followed by Gretchin and Bradley, took it to the porch and set it down. As Bradley knocked on the screen door the inner door was instantly pulled open. Then a man in a T-shirt, now clearly visible as one of the targets, pushed open the screen door and stepped out.

"Hey there," said Bradley jovially as Stanley took a step backward. "My name is Hooper, and we're a wine group from Philadelphia. At Cold Lane yesterday we did a tasting and bought two boxes of the Blush and one box of Vignoles, only to find out later that one of the Blush boxes had red in it. I don't like red, sorry, but I just don't like it." As the man stared down at the box, Bradley lifted a flap and pulled out a bottle of the wine. "See— red—all of them are red, can you believe it?"

The man grumbled, "Why bring it here?"

"That's what I said," put in Gretchin, with a note of exasperation. And lifting a hand toward Bradley, "Because he's cheap, that's why."

"I am *not* cheap," Bradley whined back at her. Then he said to the man, "When we called the vineyard, the woman gave us your address and said we could drop it off here, since I didn't want a replacement. Is that okay?"

Precluding the man's answer, Gretchin said to Bradley, "You *are* cheap," and then to the man, "He *actually* asked her if we could just leave it off at the next vineyard, have them return it to her, and then have her credit it back to his card. Know why? To save on a couple of miles in gas. Then she gave your address and said we could drop it off here."

The argument was now full blown. Bradley's face, which had reddened, wrinkled up as he whined to her, "What was wrong with my idea?"

"Because the next vineyard is her competition, stupid, think about it."

"So what?"

"So, that makes you cheap."

"I'm funding this tour. I'm not cheap."

At this point, the man, wiping a hand on his already dirty shirt, said to Bradley, "I have a woman like this. I understand."

Infuriated at this, Gretchin stomped her foot and barked at the man, "What the hell does that mean?"

"I am sorry," he returned with a shrug, "I am only saying that I understand him."

The commotion had brought another man to the door, a man with a countenance so fearsome that it showed even through the door's heavy screen. Stanley recognized him as the other target and watched him as the argument continued.

"You mean," said Gretchin heatedly, "that you sympathize with him and not me. That's what you mean, right? Man to man, and all that shit. All because I'm a woman, right? You're agreeing with him just because I'm a woman."

The other man now pushed the door open and stepped out. "What is this?" he demanded coldly, his eyes upon her. "Why is she speaking like this?"

The first man took a step backward in deference. "Mrs. Tacitti said they could leave the wine for the vineyard."

"Why?"

"She gave them the wrong wine, and they don't want to drive there for exchange."

As the second man's eyes, still on Gretchin, now showed anger, Bradley said to her, "I told you to keep out of it, now get back in the car."

She stepped off the porch, but then whirled and threw at Bradley, "You're a lousy tour guide."

His eyes grew. "I am not."

"You are."

"I am not."

"You are, asshole!" she barked. "And you're a goddamn cheapskate too!"

"Get in the car!" he shouted.

"No."

"I *am* the tour guide, and I'm telling you to get back in the car."

Stanley continued to watch the men, anticipating the appearance of others from the house.

Gretchin took two steps toward the car, then turned again. "I'll get in the car, all right, and you can find somebody else to sleep with, mister cheap ass!"

Now stepping from the porch, Bradley said, "Don't call me any more names, not one. And I wouldn't sleep with you now if you were the last whore on earth."

"Well, I wouldn't grab your dick, mister, if it was a lifeline at the edge of a cliff."

"Besides," he continued, "you would *not* be worth the price, I'll tell you that."

"Fuck you!" she screamed at him, giving him the finger.

As Bradley took another step toward her the first man said, "Just hit her."

Ignoring this, Bradley said to her, "You'd better watch your mouth. You're a disgrace. You're foul, absolutely foul. This is a public place, and these men are gentlemen. They're doing us a favor, stupid, a favor, get it? And this is the last tour for you—no more tours. Now, please just get in the car, would you?"

Connors now swung off the bike, walked quickly up to Gretchin, and took her by the arm. Stanley kept his eyes on the screen door. Inside the SUV, Packard watched carefully for others to come around the side of the house.

"Joost gat en the car," said Connors, pulling at the arm.

"Like hell I will," Gretchin shouted back at her, pulling her arm free. "Get off. Whose side are you on?"

The first man repeated, "Would somebody just hit her, please?"

But Gretchin said to everyone, "Wanna know what he asked me to do last night, d'ya wanna know?"

"Shut up!" Bradley hurled. "You're nothing but a loud-mouth, and nobody wants to hear anything you say. So, just shut your mouth."

From her vantage point in the SUV, Martina kept her eyes on Stanley. Strangely she found herself listening to the *blumm-blumm-blumm-blumm* of the Harley's idled engine, which seemed to portend the coming hailstorm.

Stanley now saw a third man appear at the door. Packard saw him, too, and got out of the SUV. Stanley, pulling the Makarov, took a step toward the third man, and then put four rapid shots through the screen and into his chest—*Pop!-Pop!-Pop!-Pop!* Instantly, Bradley spun, pulled the .45, and fired three times into the second man, blowing him backward, while Stanley threw four quick shots at the first man, who dropped, where he writhed, his arms around his middle. Stanley, now standing over him, aimed down at his head and fired. Reholstering the Makarov, he drew the Tokarev, yanked the door open and, with Bradley behind him, burst inside.

Packard, who had simply turned and walked away when the shooting began, was now unhurriedly making his way along the outside of the house. Bobbie Lee, with Connors back on the bike, now brought them to a sliding stop by the back door. Connors swung off and with a drawn .38 entered through the back door. Gretchin, retrieving her gun from the Corvette, went to the porch to guard the entrance. As she heard Connors yelling from within to check the whole house, she caught Martina, an expression of peace on her face, looking at her through the windshield of the SUV.

Two minutes passed with no abrupt sounds coming from the house. Then the front door was pushed open and Connors strode out, followed by Stanley and Bradley. Reholstering, she turned to Bradley. "What about now, preck?"

Reholstering the .45, he answered without looking at her, "There was only one. So what? What's one?"

With a gritty rumble, the Harley rolled to a stop beside the porch. Bobbie Lee planted both boots and let the engine idle. Packard, coming around from the other side of the house, simply reholstered, announced that the garage was empty except for a Toyota, climbed back into the SUV, and sat as if waiting for a ball game to come on TV.

Martina, stepping onto the porch, looked at the two dead men. Her eyes found Stanley's. "So, three?"

He nodded, then gave a slight shrug. "It tells us nothing. I agree with Bradley, not very much can be made out of an extra piece of shit."

Turning from him impatiently, she shouted toward the SUV, "Len!"

Slowly Packard opened his door and got out. As he approached the porch he growled, "What're you yellin' at me for? You don't yell at me. I'm meaner than what comes out of a dog's ass, lady. And you don't summon me, either, okay?"

Dropping her gaze, as if to calm herself, she queried, "Just one car?"

He did not answer her, but simply turned and walked back to the SUV.

She looked down again at the corpses. The first lay as if sleeping, while the second lay in a puddle of blood. "Make sure they're dead, including him in there. Then let's get the hell out of here."

Instantly Stanley aimed the Tokarev at the head of the first man, fired—*Blam-m-m-m!*—then delivered a shot to the forehead of the second— *Blam-m-m-m!*

Connors, stepping past Stanley, remarked at the blast of the Tokarev, "Fuckin' cannon. Look at the blood." Pulling the .38, she opened the door and fired twice at the head of the third man—*Plop! Plop!"*

"All right," announced Martina with finality, "it's done. Let's get out. ... See everyone at home."

Connors, turning from Bradley with disgust, jammed her gun back into its holster and stepped from the porch. Snatching up her helmet, and without bothering to pull it on, she climbed back onto her seat just as Bobbie Lee throttled up and let out the clutch. As the others were closing their doors, they heard the snarl of the motorcycle as it ran out onto the highway, then tore away.

Beams from the spring moon shone upon the highway as the Harley moved southward. The steady pounding of its powerful engine was like the beating heart of a mighty beast. The two riders were not unaware of the unity in all of this—the moonlight, the highway, the countryside, the motorcycle, the riders—a unity like that of a single candle burning.

In a small town in Pennsylvania they stopped for gas and dinner and just to loosen up from the constant heavy power-purr of the chopper. The howl of the wind was still in their heads as they entered the café and took a booth by a window. Here they shook their hair out, as if from a storm.

"I'll joost bet," offered Connors as she looked at her salad, then took up her fork, "that roidin' on t'at motorcycle without a halmet for very long would warp me fuckin' moind."

"Jist be glad you've got a good helmet, then. We've stopped at least every hour, and we've walked around a whole lot. I've been tryin' to make it easy on you."

"Et ain't been fuckin' easy."

"And hey, you watch yer language, girl. This here's Mennonite country, and they don't countenance swearin'. And this is a café, not a saloon."

"Et ain't a church neither. I once knew a nun t'at swore worse than me."

Bobbie Lee rolled her eyes, then stabbed at a piece of bell pepper. "Is that even possible? I mean, I've said it before, but really, you've got the foulest mouth of anybody I ever met in my life, girl."

"She carried a lettle bitch of a gun. She worked for the Army."

"As in Irish Republican?"

"Aye."

"Jesus! Well, your friends are meaner than mine, lady, and that's doin' somethin'. Bunch of outlaws, if you ask me. Nuns with guns—boy, that's real sick."

"Eat your denner."

Later, when the sandwiches came, Bobbie Lee queried, "Who's yer favorite artist or writer? Take yer pick."

"Where the hell'd t'at come from?"

"I jist wanna know, that's all. There's more to life than sheddin' blood. There's art, lit'ature, and symphonies. Some people might argue that those things are the only things worth fightin' for."

"Who's foightin' for anyt'ing?"

Bobbie Lee stopped chewing and let her eyes run over the shaken-out hair, the colorless eyes. "I understand what you're sayin', but some people might say it anyway."

"They'd be wastin' their toime on me."

"Look, humor me, jist give me a favorite artist. You do know a smidgen about art, right?"

"I'm not a pagan, 'course I do." And with a shrug, "Okay, maybe Van Gogh or somebody."

"Thank you. I finally got a name out of you, thank you very much. So, you're fightin' fer Van Gogh. Where'd you see his art?"

"En a book at the loibrary. . . . What about you? Who's yours?"

Momentarily, "Artist? I wouldn't know who to pick."

"Et was your fuckin' question. Why'd you ask et?"

Bobbie Lee took another bite of sandwich, then chewed slowly. "How 'bout a favorite writer? Come on, think of somethin' other'n jist killin' people."

"I dedn't kell anybody today."

"No, but you would have. And you'd be sittin' there eatin' yer food like a dog, without it botherin' you none, too."

"So would you."

"I guess you've got me there, girl. . . . And how 'bout a favorite writer?"

"Holy Mary! What're you fuckin' weth me for?"

"I don't know. I'm jist talkin' to you. Maybe I like hearin' yer voice."

Connors looked at her. "Yeats. I loike Yeats. . . . What's the difference?"

"None that I can think of."

"Then stop fuckin' weth me and eat your sandwich."

Bobbie Lee leaned closer. "Know what? I think you should come to Tinnessee and drink whiskey with me. Jack Daniel's is like sex in a bottle."

"We make some good spirits ourselves."

"Not like ours. . . . And what's yer favorite food?"

"Pizza and beer. Yours?"

Bobbie Lee drew a deep breath and let it out, puffing her cheeks. "Same."

"Anyt'ing else on your moind?"

Momentarily, "Yeah. Next time, I'm goin' in with you."

Connors pushed away the last quarter of her sandwich. "And why would you be doin' t'at? Afraid of me dyin' alone?"

Softly, "Yes."

Letting her eyes go over the chestnut hair, "Ef you could have any motorcycle en the world, what would et be?"

Bobbie Lee lifted her water glass and looked at it for a moment. "A production motorcycle?"

A shrug.

"The Sportster's pritty nice, but they've got some real trick machines out there these days. . . . Know what? I'm happy jist havin' good company to ride it with."

Now Connors lifted her glass, too, and looked at it, then at the yellow eyes. "Same here," she replied.

After following the lips as they spoke, then putting down her glass, "What's the most beautiful gun you've ever seen?"

"Couldn't pick one. Prob'ly somet'ing Cold War, I'd say. Maybe Russian or Polish, or maybe joost a Smeth. . . . I'm tired of answerin' your questions."

"I'm jist tryin' to make a fool out of you."

"Aye. And I t'ink you've done et."

"Well, like I said, it's been nice hearin' yer voice."

Martina smoothed her already smooth hair and looked over to catch her husband's profile in the glow of the dash lights. Pulling the visor down, she switched on the overhead, looked at herself in the mirror, then switched the light off again. From the back seat came the sound of Packard's heavy breathing. They had stopped for dinner and were now contentedly digesting the food and processing the alcohol. They had stopped often and were not far from home.

"You are going to say something," said Stanley, shifting the position of his hands on the wheel.

"Am I?"

"Why do you think I am loving you so much?"

"I don't know. You tell me."

Then from the back seat Packard, his head against a pillow, growled in a low voice, "I am not asleep, people."

"We will watch our language," returned the Russian.

With a grunt, keeping his eyes closed, "I'm not too fond of overhearing serious conversations, that's all."

"By *serious* you mean *intimate*, I am thinking."

But there was no response to this, and the next few minutes were spent in silence. Then Stanley said to her, "You are very quiet. You are thinking about the team, yes?"

She pulled the visor down again, without bothering to turn the light on, but then pushed it back up. "Yes," she answered softly, "I am thinking about the team. I feel frustrated that I can't protect them from the Agency, or at least from Paul."

"It is still not clear that they are trying to destroy us. The third man could easily have arrived under the radar."

"You said yourself you thought Paul was a nut."

"Yes, but we must be analyzing carefully, objectively, or we will be the psychos."

Again she looked at his profile. "Okay, but the evidence is certainly mounting. And I feel helpless to protect the team."

"You should not be worrying about this. It is not your doing. Each one of us is now responsible to be wary of Kessler, the Agency, and the intel."

"Sure. And if someone gets killed, I'm not going to feel guilty, right? Sure."

Raising the level of his voice, he queried, "What does the man in the back seat think?"

Packard roused himself and adjusted the pillow. "You don't need to ask," he answered. "I don't really care much about any of it. I just kill people for them."

She turned and looked at him. "You don't care if Paul or the Agency is actually trying to get us killed?"

"Hell no," he grunted. "That could probably be said of any company I ever worked for. And Paul, the Agency—same difference. And I don't care.

They probably *are* trying to get us killed off. It would be cheaper than giving us retirement packages. Besides, let them try, I don't care. There could've been five guys there today, who cares? Just kill five guys, that's all—five, six, whatever. But no, I don't care."

"I am not caring, either," chimed the Russian. "I am not going to be a fool, America does not love me or care about me in any way. I am being used by the Agency, that is all. It was the same for KGB guys, no one ever cared about any of them. So, what is to be expected from the Americans? The same thing. If I am not the asset, I am the liability. They do not love me. And I am crying tears, correct?"

Packard opened his eyes sleepily. "Look, society does the same thing everyday. The military's notorious for it. You could work for the post office or a grocery store—same difference. People, companies, they're all the same, they waste you, deliberately. So, get over it. If you worry about it, it'll just make your belly ache and your feet swell. Just be aware they're trying to knock us off, and let it go. And keep your gun loaded."

"Stanley grinned. "Sleep with gun, correct?"

"Kessler's afraid of us," Packard continued. "We already let him know that we're suspicious and that he'd better clean up his intel. He'll think about the rest of it, don't worry. He's afraid of us, and should be. He hand picked us, he knows we're eight dangerous people. And three of us are so goddamn good with a gun that it'd take half an army to stop us. He knows that if we turned our wrath on him, he wouldn't survive."

"Eight?" she said. "Bradley will always be on his side."

"Okay, make it seven, then," he growled, "what's the difference?"

She said nothing further about it, but tried to quell her anxiety by simply looking at the highway and the dark countryside.

Bradley turned the heat lower. He felt satisfied about the way things had gone. A mental replay of the scenes led him to the conclusion he usually arrived at, that he was more than a fair shot and had the prowess to succeed in this work. Tapping his fingers on the wheel, he began to whistle softly.

Gretchen, who had been dozing, lifted her head. "You know that bothers me."

"Sorry."

"But you knew it before you did it."

"No, I didn't."

Closing her eyes, "You did."

"But I didn't remember."

Then she put her seat back. "I'm going to try to sleep. Don't whistle."

"I said I was sorry."

"I don't care, just don't whistle."

"You're not my boss, and I'm driving *you* home. . . . Can I listen to the radio?"

"No."

For as long as he had known her he had considered her to be obnoxious. But there were positives too. For one, she smelled good. Sometimes he found her smell to be erotic. Another positive was that she was well endowed.

"Hey," he said, "that was pretty good shooting today, what do you think?"

Not bothering to open her eyes, "You're a cowboy, you're the man."

His grip on the wheel tightened He hated it when she teased him. "Admit it," he said, "a .45's hard to control, but I didn't miss."

"Nerves of steel. You'll have to buy yourself a cigar."

"Might just do that."

"Yeah, and get a grown-up to smoke it for you."

He ground his teeth. "Are you jealous?"

"Nope."

"I think you are. You didn't get to do much today, did you?"

"Remember Carlysle? Let's see, what did *you* do? You drove the car. You sat in your leather seat, played with the temperature control, and then drove to pick me up after I had done the job."

"Yeah, that's true."

With her eyes still closed, "No, no, don't try sensitivity, it just doesn't fit."

"But I can be sensitive. You never give me a chance."

"I've seen what you do with a chance." And with a weary sigh, "I'd like to get a little sleep, okay?"

"Just trying to make conversation. You never just talk, do you?"

"Not with you, Bradley. Jesus!"

"Why not?"

"Because you're not sensitive, asshole."

"Come on, keep me awake here. It's just conversation, okay? What's wrong with a little talk?"

She opened her eyes and raised her head. "You're sleepy?"

"Yeah."

"And I'm supposed to do what about that?"

With a shrug, "I don't know. Read something to me maybe."

Contemptuously, "I'll pass, bud."

"Or just talk a little."

"I'm doing that. And it's not easy."

"We're almost home, and I'm very tired, Gretchin. Can't you do a little more talking to keep me awake, just for a little while?"

"I'll pass."

"You'll be sorry. I'm feeling groggy."

"Okay," she said, raising her seat up, "pull in for coffee, first place."

"Can't be sociable, huh?"

"Not with you, dick. Just stay awake till you see something, but then pull in."

CHAPTER 16

Lancaster County

It was not until just before noon that Connors awoke. Instinctively she slid her hand under the pillow and withdrew the .38. Aiming it at the bright window, she recalled the time she had done the same thing but had pulled the trigger just for the hell of it, blowing the window out. Tossing the gun onto the bed covers, she turned over and grabbed the doll from the night table.

"You should've spent the noight weth me," she whispered. "Bet you were cold." After pulling the covers up again, she hugged the doll with one hand and reached for the gun with the other. "There's nothin'," she whispered in the doll's ear, "loike bein' safe en your bed."

When her phone buzzed, she pulled it from the charging cord, opened it, and read, *Hey. Sleeping late?* Quickly she texted back, *You had breakfast yet?* Moments later she read, *No. Ssee you there in few minutes.*

Fifteen minutes later she sat before a bowl of fruit salad and a cup of black coffee.

"Hey there," said Bobbie Lee, tucking flannel shirt tails into her jeans and taking a seat. "Lord, did I sleep! I mean, I could hardly git off the bike when we rolled in. I think I could've slept all day."

"Why dedn't you?"

"Good question, girl, but here I am. I feel like I've slept in a dumpster."

"You pretty much look et. You moight not know et, but you can brush hair when et gats loike t'at."

"I've heard about doin' that. Guess I'll have to find my brush. But I'm from the hill country, and we don't do much to our hair in the mornin'. Hey, look at this coffee, perfect, jist what I'm after."

Sticking her head through the kitchen doorway, Maggie queried, "How about some fresh pancakes, you two?"

"Oh, I've died," responded Bobbie Lee, "and gone to heaven. Please, Maggie, that would be great."

Connors sipped her coffee, waited until Maggie was back in the kitchen, then said, "I gave the doll a name."

"Yeah? Gonna make me guess?"

"Bobbie."

"Nice name, girl."

As the agent wheeled them up the Estate's long driveway toward the fountain Kessler caught sight of Bradley washing his Corvette in front of the stables. For some reason the scene made him feel sick, and he wanted to cover his eyes. But he continued to watch as Bradley, garden hose in hand and grinning, happily rinsed suds from the gaudy car all as if it was a big yellow dog.

"Joe," he muttered as they rounded the fountain, "why does God countenance fools like that?"

"Don't know, sir. But that's a great car. Wish I had one."

"Do you, Joe? And do you wish you had a hose like that and a big stupid grin like that?"

The agent shut the engine off. "He waved to you, sir. Didn't you see it?"

"I did, Joe, I did. I just couldn't bring myself to wave back."

"Do you think he'll be hurt?"

"Probably not, Joe. . . . Come on, let's go in."

"Well, now," said Maggie, presenting the refreshments, "here we are again, and I hope everyone will find things satisfactory. Help yourselves, please. Paul?"

He had been watching her push the cart and now stared up at her. "Yes, Maggie, certainly. I would enjoy a good cup of your tea, yes. And one of those cakes too, I think. Did you bake these things, Maggie, can I ask?"

"I did, yes," she replied, filling a cup for him. "But it isn't much, just a few treats."

After everyone had taken something from the cart and was seated, Maggie took one of the cakes and a cup of tea for herself and sat down next to her husband. She felt her face redden as he gave her hand a pat, but was glad that he was not above showing his affection for her.

"I suppose," said Kessler, clacking his cup and saucer, "we should get started." After giving his hands a rub together, he chuckled awkwardly, and continued, "I am embarrassed, to say the least, that I have to confess to everyone the failure of the Agency. But I will do it. I think you all know that I will always be the first to admit failure. And frankly, to lay it all out on the table, the Agency has failed us again. Their intel let us down, didn't it?"

Connors cocked her head and replied in an obviously sarcastic tone, "And you dedn't know a t'ing about et, did you?"

He frowned, as if hurt. "Of course not, Kelly, and I'm terribly sorry about it. And I'm embarrassed. I don't know what else to say. I'm certainly glad none of you was hurt." And dropping his gaze, he added, "It's miraculous how you've all avoided being hurt, considering the bad intel we've received. Maybe you're all just—lucky."

"Know what," said Bobbie Lee, "I'm gittin' me another one of them cakes. Maggie, this shit's first rate."

He watched as she went to the cart, lifted the cover, snatched up a cake, crammed half of it into her mouth, then returned to her seat. It was such behavior that made him doubt whether he had been wise in choosing her for the team. He could boast of her prowess in the field, but there were moments when he wished she possessed even a little social refinement.

"Okay, Paul," said Stanley, "you are being sorry for this, but it does not seem that you are promising us better intel."

With a shrug, "Well, I have to say that you are correct."

The Russian did not reply immediately, but took a sip from his cup. Then he said, "When KGB wanted to get rid of someone, they just did it, they did not wait for it to happen. Are you waiting for it to happen? Are you waiting for our luck to run out?"

"No, of course not. That's ridiculous, Stanley. Why would I do that? That's a terrible thing to say, and frankly I'm a little offended."

With a chuckle, "Offended?"

"Well, sure. You said it so easily and in front of everyone. Think of all I've done for you guys. You're my team, you mean a lot to me. Stanley, it was just a terrible thing to say."

"Et would be," put in Connors, "ef et wasn't fuckin' true."

Suddenly Packard smacked his lips and said, "Hey, guess what, everybody, Maggie and I are going to Florida. We're retiring. We're going to stop and just play in the sun. How about that?"

Recovering from the abrupt interruption, Kessler offered, "Well, I'm thrilled, Len. Congratulations. I wish both of you all the best. That sounds great, just great."

"So, I'm not going to see you in my rearview mirror?"

Kessler stared at him. "Nobody's going to stop you from retiring, Len. You and Maggie will go with the Agency's blessing."

"And yours?"

"Certainly. You both have my blessing."

"Ah, ain't that sweet?" said Bobbie Lee. "Ain't that jist so goddamn sweet? If we survive the

Agency's bad intel, we can get Paul's blessin' and retire to Florida."

Here the sidekick agent stopped chewing his cake and looked at her.

But Bradley said, "The Agency hasn't done anything wrong. It's all just circumstances, that's all."

With this, the agent resumed chewing.

Kessler put his hands together. "Thank you, Brad, for the good common sense. And listen, everyone, the intel was goofy, that's all, you have my word on that, and I wouldn't lie to you. And, Len, Maggie, again, I wish you all the best in your plans. I hope you enjoy Florida. I've been there, and I liked it a lot."

Martina cleared her throat gently, then said, "I'm sure we all have the choice of continuing with the Agency or not. And we all look forward to retirement."

"If," said Gretchin, "their shitty intel doesn't get us killed first."

"Gretchin," replied Kessler sorrowfully, "I'm sorry about the intel, and I suspect it has done a lot to erode your trust in us."

She was incredulous. "*Trust?* God Almighty! Are you serious? There's nothing to erode, Paul. I don't trust you or the Agency one goddamn little bit."

He shut his eyes, as if to emphasize his sincerity. "I know you don't, Gretchin. But I want you to trust us. You're a good agent. You're good with this team. I only hope that both the Agency and I can work harder to win your trust. That's . . . well, that's all I can do at this point."

Stanley uncrossed his legs and looked at the toes of his boots, then directly at Kessler. He spoke quietly. "I never trusted you or CIA, even the little bit, and I never will. I know from my experience that this world of espionage, as it is called, is a world of reptiles and slime and shadows. *We* are reptiles, dragons that work for you and CIA. As team members we might love each other as comrades or not, but we will never love the system." He followed this with a shrug. "But all of this is coming with the territory, as they say. So, I can accept it and continue to work with you. But trust you? I think not—any more than you trust me."

With a chuckle, "Well said, Mr. Osipov, well said. And I can live with that. Good." Then he sat back and smiled as he looked around at all of them. "I hope all of you can give the Agency a second chance. I'll try to get better intel out of them, I will. But in the end, I guess we'll just have to work with what they give us."

In vain he waited for some response. Finally his eyes fell upon Connors. Here there could be a real problem, he knew, for this was simply the most dangerous woman he had ever known. And so far, one of the luckiest. How in God's name had she and her girlfriend here simply dealt with those two guys? No, intel had not slipped up. They knew the guys were there and that they were professionals. Now as he looked at her he felt an eerie fear creep into his mind. He had never known any man or woman more dangerous than she. He could not even imagine a fitting label for her. As an instrument of death she was uncompromisingly lethal. At length he simply looked away from her and said, "Kelly, are you okay going on with everything? I will try to get more reliable intel, I promise."

"Oh, aye," she came back almost casually.

Swallowing in spite of himself, he looked at her again, then at Bobbie Lee and said, "Ms. Henry?"

Balling her fists and watching the muscles in her forearms ripple, she replied, "I'm in if Killy's in. But you might ask the Agency not to throw any more of them pro bodyguards at us like they did in Cape May. Them two shits could have ruined my shrimp dinner."

With difficulty he forced from his mind images from the photos the cleanup crew had included with their report—the ghastly scene of the women and bodyguards as they lay by their blanket, their faces and heads shot, bleeding into the sand. "I'll relay the message, Ms. Henry."

"So," said the Russian somewhat abruptly, "the team is continuing, correct?"

Kessler looked at him. "Well, I should hope so, Stanley, yes." And looking around at them all, "I'd like Martina to continue on as team leader, of course. She's a cool thinker, and I like her wisdom. I need Kelly to lead with the trigger, but I need Martina behind the switchboard, as it were. . . . Yes, it's fine with me if everything goes on as it did before. I'm happy. I think you all do great work, and the Agency thinks so, too. In fact, that's kind of why I'm here today. I have been told that the team is now considered by the Agency to be primary, even somewhat indispensable."

Martina was not alone in catching the glimmer of disappointment in his eyes.

"And Len, Maggie," he added, "what can I say but good luck to you both. We'll miss you."

CHAPTER 17

Fernandina Beach, Florida

Maggie put down her letter and raised the armrests of her chair. The flaps of the umbrella that blocked the October sun wavered in the breeze. She looked up and then down the stretch of white sand, then caught sight of him. He would not arrive for another few minutes, she estimated, for she could see that the front of his T-shirt, which he had stretched out to form a bucket, was full of shells, and that he was still collecting. Closing her eyes, she took in another deep breath of air luxuriously salted by the gentle breakers.

"Brought you a bunch of shells," he said, dropping to his knees. From his shirt he dumped the shells onto the blanket beside her chair. "To add to the collection. Maybe we'll glue 'em on the wall. It'd be pretty, don't you think?"

She squinted at him. His short beard seemed improved by the overexposure to salt and sand. But that was just her opinion, and her opinion could not be trusted, she would be the first to admit, for it was made inadmissible by the fact that she loved this man Leonard Packard. She watched as he lifted the cooler lid and retrieved an iced bottle. It seemed that she found nearly everything he did to be a visual joy. Then she began to read again the letter from Martina.

"Want a beer," he queried.

"Sure, that would be good, Mr. Packard."

She followed his movements as he removed the cap, wiped the top with a towel, handed her the bottle, then got another for himself. She knew he would not wipe the top of his own bottle, just as she knew that his defense if challenged would be that he liked a little grit with his beer.

"What'd she want," he asked, but then said, "Hey, know what this stuff is? The greatest stuff in the world, right there in your hand."

"She wants us to come back north."

"As in move?"

"She says the new range is twice as big as what they asked for, with air control."

"Guess he was sucking up to them."

"She says the new pool's just waiting for me."

He let the liquid surround his tongue, then swallowed. Pointing the bottle toward the water, he said, "Look at this. Who would leave this? Hell, getting here was like getting to heaven. And tonight we're ordering out for pizza. And she's inviting us back to a farm? Really?"

"It's not a farm, Lenny. That's not fair."

He replied by simply tipping the bottle up and taking another swig.

"But that's what she says," she continued. "She says she and Bobbie Lee have been trading off on the cooking all summer. She says everyone misses my cooking, Len—*mine*. She says they especially miss my pies. And Bobbie Lee's no third-rate cook, so you know what they're saying."

"That you're the best cook in the galaxy?"

With a smile, "Something like that."

He waited for her sweet sigh, then said, "I guess you miss Connors' language."

"Well, yours isn't much cleaner."

"Thanks much."

"You bet."

He put the bottle down and steadied it. "Look, sweetheart, we're older, old enough to retire, and that's what we've done. What's wrong with that? Just let it go. Enjoy the sand dollars and conks, the beach, the water, the goddamn pizza. We're retired. Now just let it go."

"I'm not a moralist, you know that. But Martina needs us, they all need us, or she wouldn't have said it."

He turned to face her. "Look, dear, sweetheart, I have spent most of my life killing people. I stopped counting them when I was still young. I've got so much blood on my hands, I couldn't wash it off in the ocean. Now, fortunately, I've lived long enough to retire. I like waking up with you every morning and taking my time at it. I like the beach and the relaxed life we have here. So, just let it go—please. Tell her no."

She looked out to where the little breakers were foaming. "I know what you're talking about, Mr.

Packard. I have an appreciation for it, myself. But—"

"But what?" he growled.

"Well, . . . they miss my pies, they miss my cooking, my hospitality. That means a lot to me, too."

"Hospitality? Hell, nobody ever came around but that goddamn Kessler."

"Not fair, Lenny."

Giving his head a shake, he said, "Your pies? You're a brilliant woman. You're a wonderful photographer. You're beautiful and you're sexy. And I'm sure you were probably a great teacher. I wouldn't be a good judge of that, I guess, since I always hated teachers—bunch of sadists, if you ask me. But you're a great woman, and now you've retired. Don't you like retirement? Look at all this here, the sand, the seashells, the sunlight. You spent your life teaching school and working for the CIA. That's two careers. Great, wonderful. Now you're retired, as you should be. You're a retiree, you've got a little piece of heaven before you get there, so why give it up? Just keep drinking the alcohol and eating the pizza and let it go."

"But it *would* be retirement, the way she describes it. I wouldn't be going out on projects, I'd be supporting the team from behind the scenes. I want to be retired and work behind the scenes, what's wrong with that?"

He gave her a hard look, then took a swig from the bottle. "It's cold there. Pennsylvania's colder than a pocketful of bullets. It's really nice here. You hate the cold, you've said that a hundred times. What about that?"

"I know," she replied, reaching to touch the stubble on his gritty cheek, "but I'll have you."

"And that's another thing. What exactly would *I* do, clean the goddamn toilets?"

"Well, I was thinking you could run the gun range and do gunsmithing for the team. You'd like that, wouldn't you? Maybe sometimes you could go out on a project. I wouldn't want you to go every time, but occasionally wouldn't hurt, just for fun. Come on, Lenny, please. I could swim every day in the pool, if I wanted."

"Not for long. Swimmin' there would be like swimmin' in a bucket of ice."

"And we could even come back here for vacation."

"We'll have to. Hell, it snows there in October."

Lancaster County

After tossing her empty cup into the recycling bin, Gretchin reached into her purse and gripped the rubber butt of the .38. Then she touched the 9mm nestled at the other end of the purse. For any fast work, she must instinctively go for the Smith, but for everything else, the Glock.

With hearing protectors squarely in place, she entered the barrier room, then stepped into the range. The concussion from Bradley's .45 seemed as menacing as ever. Stepping up behind him, she waited for the magazine change. When he turned around to reload and had grinned at her, she wondered why at forty-four he should seem to be so young. She also wondered whether he would ever find her attractive. When he's sixty I'll be seventy-two, she thought. Then she stopped all her thinking and simply watched him.

Moving to the next lane, she realized that she was not flinching at the concussion of the heavy .45's. After taping a target into place, she threw the toggle switch, sent the hanger downrange, and stopped it at the thirty-foot mark. Her target hung clean beside his, which was riddled. She pretended not to be alarmed as one of his casings hit her on the cheek. She waited for him to finish the mag, then drew the Glock from the holster in her cross-slung purse, leveled it, and emptied it downrange in a fury. When she turned to look at him, she only saw the white teeth of his boyish grin, a grin that had never failed to make her mad. After reholstering the Glock, she looked up at him again, and for some reason, found herself smiling at him and searching his eyes. Then she nodded toward her target, most of whose center she had blown out.

When she left he followed her and in the kitchen asked her why she had been friendly to him. But she refused to answer him, and impishly drank from the faucet and wiped her mouth with her hand. Then he took hold of her arm and asked her to kiss him.

"Don't ask me to kiss you," she said. "If you want to kiss me, kiss me, stupid." But when he simply released her arm, she said, "I have to take a shower, I have gunpowder all over me." And when he just looked at her, she asked, "Want to wash my back?"

Then she left the kitchen, and again he followed her.

During dinner that evening Martina made the announcements that Maggie and Leonard had agreed to return to the team and that Paul Kessler was being replaced. He had called her earlier with the news. He assured her that although he was being reassigned to another area the Agency had found his service to be fully acceptable and often exemplary. The team's new contact had not been chosen.

"There wasn't much else to the call," she said, allowing her eyes to rest for an instant upon each of them. "Then he just said goodbye, and that was it. . . . He did not sound happy."

Stanley pulled at his ear. "Well, I am telling the truth, CIA is nicer than KGB."

Bradley pushed his plate and put both elbows on the table. "Get over it, Osipov, it's the FSB and the SVR now. You're living in the past, bub."

"Of course this is true, I admit it, and all the people I know who are still KGB are imaginary."

"I still say he was a good guy. And I'm gonna miss him. He looked really neat in a windbreaker."

"Sort of *government*," added Bobbie Lee.

But Gretchin had rolled her eyes. "*Really neat,* Bradley?" she repeated. "That's how you saw him?"

Her tone, however, had been different, almost kind, so that the other women took note of it. Even Bradley seemed surprised, but then began tapping his water glass with his fork. When she told him to stop, he obeyed, a submissive look on his face.

"I think," offered Bobbie Lee, "they were up to his plan to git us, and they wanted to stop him before we did. Now, what's ever'body think of them apples?"

Connors, giving a macabre chuckle, said, "I was gattin' ready, I can say et for a fact. I was gattin' ready to gun t'at fucker down pairsonally. . . . And maybe some of his friends too."

Avoiding her gaze, Bradley said, "That sounds like a threat, Kelly."

But the gaze was steady, and the reply cold. "I never t'reaten people."

"Really?" he returned, now looking at her. "Because you threatened me, I'm pretty sure. At least, I took it as a threat—something about smearing my guts on the wall."

"T'at wasn't a t'reat, t'at was a promise."

"Okay, okay," put in Martina, "for whatever reason, Paul Kessler is gone and we're getting someone else. That's all we need to know right now. He said the new contact would be getting in touch with us. . . . So, is everyone in favor of having Maggie back to take care of the household, and Leonard to handle the range and weapons maintenance?"

"Totally perfect," replied the Russian. "They are both excellent people. KGB would kill to have such people on their side." And glancing at Bradley, "But of course, since KGB does not exist anymore, it is not an issue."

Bradley returned the look. "You know, Osipov, you sure sound like you miss your comrades. Why don't you just buy yourself a one-way ticket back to Moscow?"

"Because," put in Gretchin, "he's got Martina. And he's got us too."

But again, her tone lacked its usual acidic character. She had corrected him without trying to hurt him. Connors and Bobbie Lee exchanged smiles at this, and Martina raised her eyebrows. Aware of the scrutiny, Gretchin flushed pink. And then an image, flashing across her mind, of his hands washing her back and moving down her body, turned the pink to a definite red.

Bradley only muttered back to her, "Sure." But his heart began to race as he recalled how she had turned toward him in the shower, soap running down between her breasts. Quickly he dropped his gaze and stared at his plate. Then the whole scene filled his mind, of her arching her back as the soap was washed away, of her toweling herself off, and of her leading him to the bed and then spreading her legs for him.

"Good," said Martina, with a definite note of finality. "And we'll all look forward to meeting the new contact. I'll let you know."

CHAPTER 18

Nothing more was heard from the Agency until late in December, when a call came through to Martina from a woman introducing herself as Mary Coldgrave, the new contact. Martina listened intently, to the pleasant, naturally suave voice, but could not help wondering why the woman had called three days before Christmas. Following the short conversation, she had the distinct impression she had been talking to an aristocrat.

But if the woman had thought little of calling so close to a holiday, she apparently thought less of arriving on Christmas Eve. As the Jaguar rolled up to the Estate's front door, it was obvious to Maggie, peering from behind a curtain, that this Mary Coldgrave had driven herself. And when the door of the sleek green car was opened, Maggie watched with interest as the woman stepped out in the regalia of a fashion queen, glanced around at the frost-covered grounds, then drew from the sumptuous interior a long wool coat and pushed the door home with a gorgeously leather-gloved hand.

Not waiting for the bell, Maggie opened the front door, then the storm door, and greeted the woman with a broad smile. "Mary? Hi, come in, please."

The woman stepped in, handed over the coat, which she had not put on, but did not remove her gloves, and said simply, "It is blustery out. I was driving through the wilderness, I think."

"Yes, it is, quite. Now, come in, please. Everyone is waiting for you. We are all anxious to meet the new person."

All eyes were upon this Mary Coldgrave as she followed Maggie into the living room to be formally introduced. Her splendid clothes made her entrance impressive enough, but her unusual beauty made it overwhelming. Even more, there was a certain sensuality about the woman that seemed effortlessly to communicate with everyone in the room. All stood as she came in, and Martina stepped forward to wait for Maggie's introduction.

"Martina, everyone," Maggie announced gracefully, "please meet Mary Coldgrave."

"Yes, hi," said the woman, looking around at them and offering a pleasant smile. After shaking Martina's hand, she added, "I think I know everyone, from your files, of course. Charming group. Thanks for having me. And I suppose I should say Merry Christmas."

She was politely self-assured as she took a seat and received a cup of tea and a slice of Maggie's holiday cornbread upon a china plate. Her hair was brown, shoulder length, her teeth were astoundingly white against her red lipstick, and her left eye independently looked out to the side, a feature that only made her seem more beautiful, more sensual. All of this immediately put her at a distance, until she spoke.

"I'm so glad," she said, "you agreed to see me on such short notice and during the holidays too. . . . I'm Mary, I'm your new contact, and there will be no one between you and me. You can call me at any time and for any reason. I have read all the files thoroughly. You are an amazing team, none of you has been hurt, except for Kelly Connors, who was wounded by Leonard Packard. Well, each of you has an exceptional record. Are there any questions so far?"

Martina sat forward. "Could you tell us a little about yourself?"

"Well, yes. I'm from New York City originally. I'm from wealth frankly, so, you understand, it was posh New York. I'm thirty-four years old, I speak my mind, and I like to drink. So, how is that, how did I do?" This was followed by a sumptuous smile, one that, especially under such arresting, disparate eyes, might drive a woman to jealousy or nudge a man into an erection.

Martina, lifting her chin, took note not only that the woman was perhaps too candid, but that she had strangely not removed her gloves. Maggie, blinking repeatedly, merely cleared her throat politely. Gretchin, watching the woman's body language, threw a glance now and then in Bradley's direction. Neither Connors nor Bobbie Lee seemed to care much for any of it. But the men, who had had the woman undressed the moment she walked into the room, all sat watching as the gloved hands expressed the heart and soul of the female beast.

"By the way," continued Coldgrave cheerily, "might I have a drink? The tea is so good, thank you, but yes, I think I need a drink."

After the general silence that followed this, Maggie replied, "Of course. What would you like?"

"Well, I don't want to drive drunk—they don't let you do that anymore, I understand—but, well, what is everyone else having?"

Another general silence. Then Maggie offered, "We have a lot of different craft beers, if that would do. They're very good, especially on a night like this."

"'There's only the Cutty Sark left en the cabinet, ef yous want wheskey," said Connors. "Aye, I drank the rast."

"But the beer would be splendid," was the response.

"Would a lager do, to start?"

A sensuous, then sensual, nearly seductive smile. "Oh, that would be lovely. It will keep me awake for the trip home."

As Maggie took orders for drinks and then left for the kitchen, Coldgrave seemed to lapse into a kind of melancholy. But soon, with a tall glass of the lager in hand, for it was only in preparation of this that she had removed the gloves, she seemed distinctly to brighten and to become cheerful again. All her attention seemed now devoted to the beer. Delicately she first put the foam just under her nose to appreciate its bouquet, then she simply tipped the glass and continued to drink until half its contents were gone.

"How is the lager, Mary?" asked Maggie after distributing beers to the others.

"Very nice," was the reply.

And then shortly, "Would you like another? Perhaps a porter?"

A broad smile. "Yes, Maggie, that would be wonderful, thank you. I must apologize for my consumption, you understand. I don't really become drunk, you know, I just sort of float."

A few minutes later, a glass of the porter in hand, Coldgrave straightened herself a little and said, "I am glad you all have such a nice place here. And I understand the range is fully operational. The pool, of course, will be delightful in the summertime. . . . Do you swim, Kelly?"

With a snicker, "Maybe a lettle."

"Do you wear a bikini?"

"Sometoimes. Sometoimes I wear nothin'."

Coldgrave crossed her legs at this, then looked around, her right eye moving over the team. Bobbie Lee Henry—quite the Rebel, so to speak. Daring feats. Extreme prowess with weapons and nearly acrobatic on a motorcycle. Incredible courage. Fiercely loyal to her own brand of neo-Southern Confederacy. Martina—Nazi parents. Objective, wise, diplomatic, thoroughly competent and trustworthy to lead the team. Her husband Stanley Osipov—confusing mix of politics, a sort of democratic Communist. Wears cowboy boots, but is no would-be American. Interesting and perhaps dangerous connections with old KGB. Has an artistic mind, takes nude photos of Martina.

Gretchin Wheeler—recklessly free spirit and a loud mouth of the first order. Obnoxiously disrespectful. Deemed to be unreliable outside the dynamic of the team. Bradley Hopkins—red, white and blue to the bone. Unswerving loyalty to the Agency. Obviously sleeps with Ms. Wheeler. Margaret Swift-Jones—intelligent, precise, objective, with an old-world mentality. Retired but now working again for the Agency, along with her newly wedded husband, the notorious Leonard Packard. The file had been explicit about him, describing him as a spreader of death. Crotchety, at best, otherwise genuinely mean. She took more of the porter as she considered him, this professional, this kind of off-the-charts natural killer. She looked into his face as he chatted with Maggie, a cup of tea in his hand, guns puffing his old sportcoat like they were so much eiderdown. Jesus. And then there was Kelly Connors—the report had been pithy. Acquired out of Ireland via a secret deal. Wretched past of blood and gore. Judged to be one of the most capable killers ever encountered by the CIA. Fearless to the point of being unearthly. Considered extremely dangerous even to the Agency itself. Her only known objects of loyalty were her mother and the Irish Republic.

Then impulsively she said to Martina, "As I say, I don't want to drive intoxicated. I don't want to have some trooper ask me for something special, if you know what I mean."

With a blink of incredulity, "Yes, yes, I think I do."

"But I'm kidding, of course. I do make jokes."

"But you are certainly welcome to stay here, if you like. We have plenty of space, and you can have a room to yourself."

Delicately brushing the hair from her cheek, she held up her glass and said, "Two if you're driving, three if you're biking, four if you're walking, I think, is the rule. . . . I never really become intoxicated, you understand, but it is the holiday time and others are out on the roads in no condition to drive."

A smile. "Oh, yes, stay here, would you? We'd love to have you."

"Well, I suppose I could, if you wouldn't mind. Wouldn't want to run the Jag into a truck. I don't want to inconvenience you, but that would be great." With her glass she swept the room. "This is all very pleasant. I like your decorations. They're subtle, quite tasteful. Gretchin's the artist, I understand."

"Yes. She painted the snowflakes."

"And do you have a pumpkin?"

Martina looked at her. "A pumpkin, Mary?"

Hesitating, "Uh—you know, I think I mean a tree. Do you have a tree?"

"We do, yes. And Gretchin made some of the decorations for it."

"I like a tree and mistletoe and things like that. I enjoy all the holidays immensely, Halloween, Thanksgiving, and even, what is that, Labor Day. Yes, Labor Day is nice. That's the one for candy and chocolate."

"That might be Valentine's Day."

"Oh yes, right." And gazing around, "Christmas parties are a wonderful diversion, don't you think?"

By now there was general chatter in the room, so that Martina felt compelled to clear her throat politely and query, "Mary, could I ask you, is there a new project you want us to get ready for?"

Coldgrave lifted her eyebrows, which rendered the effect of the disparate eyes even more striking, and then, as if emerging from a brief trance, said, "Oh, yes, that's right. I do, yes. Thank you, Martina."

"Surely. And would you care for another drink? A pale ale, perhaps?"

"I would, yes, thank you." But with a smile, "Wouldn't want to bulge the tummy though. Would there be anything stronger but less effervescent?"

Wondering why beautiful people always complained of their looks, and thin people, their weight, Martina replied, "I think there's some gin, if that would suit?"

A few minutes later, after Maggie had brought the glass of gin on ice, Coldgrave raised a hand to get the general attention, cleared her throat, and said, "Now, everyone, I must tell you, the Agency is very happy that the operation of this team has been so efficient. It is only hoped that 2012 will prove to be another successful year. It will be the Year of the Dragon, as you might know, which certainly means it could be a lucky year. In any case, there are two brothers who are involved in supplying weapons to terrorists of some sort—I don't really know about them, the terrorists, that is. In any case, the Agency has issued an order to put them down—the two men, that is. And that's your new project. How does that sound?" She followed this by drawing in some of the cold gin, then swallowing appreciatively.

There was a general silence, then Connors asked, "What're we talkin' about here? Joost where are t'ese two fuckers?"

Coldgrave stared at her. The reports had certainly been accurate about this one, she considered. Quite the specimen of the profane. Momentarily she replied, "They are in this country actually."

Bradley frowned. "That's my question—when do we get to travel? You know, go international? We're not even supposed to be operating inside the U.S., are we, Mary?"

Thoughtfully she took a sip of the gin, then replied, "Think of it this way, if you have to, Bradley, the United States *is* international. That should be explanation enough, I should think. Who cares whether the enemy brings it here or we take it there? I know *I* don't." When he did not reply, she continued, "But if we could focus, Mr. Hopkins."

This he did not like and showed it by looking her up and down.

"Intel," she continued, "expects them to leave the country soon. They live in France, the south of France. Anyway, they are in North Carolina, of all places. They have purchased a small boat and spend their time fishing—with poles, I assume."

"Poles?" repeated Bobbie Lee. "You mean, fishin' rods an' tackle an' stuff?"

"Yes, that's correct, I think. I am not an expert on mundane things."

Stanley let his eyes move over her. He did not, himself, harbor resentment toward aristocrats, as his father Alexy would have done, but if pressed, he would have to confess they irritated him. It was their bearing, their attitude, the very words they used, and especially the inflection in their voice.

"Anyway," she continued, "just don't let them leave the country. I'm sure you'll find a way to prevent that. I'll send you a couple of photos and more info on the project soon."

Bradley dropped his foot from his knee. "Are all the rules the same as they were with Paul? I mean, about not using smart phones or computers on the project? I'm just asking."

"Um, yes, Bradley," she replied, "I think they are. Kessler had a few good ideas, you know. That was one of them. He envisioned the team only as being *in the raw*, as he put it. And I think it should stay that way, too, sort of natural in its creativity. Besides, if it isn't broken, let's not try to repair it, right?"

Wrinkling his nose, he said, "Sure, right, I wouldn't think of changing anything."

"But you did think of it, didn't you? Otherwise, you wouldn't have asked, I should think."

"Sure, right," he stammered. "That's right, yep. Anyway, everything's okay with me. I'm all set. And the project sounds great, it does."

Gretchin put her forefinger up. "I have a question. Why was Paul reassigned? What happened, if you can tell us?"

She looked at her for a moment. "It was because of his wife. Suicide. Sleeping pills. They found her in her car at a turnpike rest stop. . . . It happens."

After a moment of general silence, Martina asked, "Is there anything more you can tell us about it?"

"Not really. It was ugly. Suicide usually is. It's a solution, but it's ugly. Besides, as you no doubt observed, he was somewhat obsessive about his theories. I suppose it must be acknowledged by everyone who worked with him that he was a little *off*, as it were. But then, who of us isn't?"

Maggie, smiling sweetly, returned, "Yes."

Following another sip of gin, "He was correct about a lot of things. He was spot-on about the creativity of this team. Whether that creativity is replicable or simply phenomenal is arguable. But yes, your work has proven to be, to say the least, creative. As a matter of fact, it might be argued scientifically that the team's creativity has something to do with it's luck."

Bradley frowned. "Luck?"

"Uh, yes, right, I should have been specific. Not luck as to your abilities, but as to your survival, that none of you has been hurt, at least not appreciably."

Martina then queried, "Is he getting along in his reassignment?"

"It seems like, yes. At least, I've heard that he is."

With a nod, "We're glad."

The reply was cool. "I'm sure you can say that perfunctorily, but I am aware that most of you suspected him of questionable motives as to the team."

Aware that eyes had shifted to him, Bradley began playing with his shoestring.

It was Maggie who responded, "We did, Mary, yes, and for the good reason that the evidence pointed to it."

But Bradley said, "You people speak for yourselves. I always said he was a good guy. I'll let it go, but that's what I said."

"And you'll stick to it, right?" quipped Gretchin.

He let go of the shoestring. "Yes, I will, thank you."

Coldgrave, as if to draw the discussion about Kessler to a close, then said, "Good. It's good to discuss things. Thank you all. . . . Now, Martina, I will stay, yes. If I might just see the room now, please, that would be great." And pulling on her gloves, she stood.

After Maggie had showm Coldgrave to her room, she remarked to Martina over hot chocolate in the kitchen that she wouldn't drive, either, under the influence of so much alcohol. As they had both kept count of the glasses of beer and then gin the woman had consumed, they scowled over how much high society must be used to drinking and remarked how she had not seemed even to approach tipsiness.

"Those clothes," said Martina, "the coat, the dress, the shoes, you're talking thousands probably. Maybe five thousand or more just for the coat, that kind of thing."

"You don't have to tell me, dear," replied Maggie, taking a sip of the chocolate. "Lenny couldn't keep his eyes off her, and I don't mean for the the clothes."

"Neither could Stanley."

"God! The woman's got sex appeal—and knows it, I'm afraid. But I wonder what she's got at the core, what she can do professionally."

Martina wrinkled her nose. "What's with the gloves?"

"I connected it with the alcohol, myself. What she said about Paul, though, seemed to neutralize our suspicions, don't you think?"

"But had it been calculated to do so?"

In the morning, after everyone else had been up for an hour or more, Coldgrave made her appearance in the dining room to announce her departure. Neither the short-notice stay nor the alcohol had diminished the glamour, and the woman seemed ready for any new task that might beset any aristocrat. Her hair perfect, her lipstick perfect, her gloves pulled snug and tight, she looked around at them, with the air of an approving general, before she spoke.

"I see you are having a good time," she said. "I'll just take a bite to eat, if you don't mind, and yes, some coffee."

And perhaps a glass of beer with your breakfast and a flask of vodka for the road, Maggie wanted to add.

"And then I'll be off," Coldgrave said cheerily, pulling out a chair. "I'm headed for New York. Family, you know, and I must be there. But it will be fun. Just hope the Jag gets me there."

Stanley, his hands around a mug of coffee, could not help rolling his eyes at this. Martina cleared her throat. Maggie left for the kitchen.

"I'll only have one pancake, if you don't mind," continued Coldgrave, clearly enjoying herself, "and the coffee black, of course, to keep me awake on the highways. Mustn't fall asleep. That's as frowned upon now as driving drunk, and for good reason, I'm sure."

Gretchin sniffed and then offered, "Merry Christmas, Mary."

Coldgrave beamed. "Oh yes, I guess it is Christmas. Merry Christmas, Gretchin, everyone, happy holidays."

It was then, observing her charm, her one eye out of touch and the other twinkling, that Stanley felt an odd twinge of coldness. Years before, he had encountered a KGB woman who used her sweet demeanor to distract her victims before she brutally put them to death.

After cutting through her pancake, Coldgrave looked up and said sweetly, "Just to take up a little from last evening, I wanted to mention that the weapons should pretty much stay as they are, with allowance for variations to accommodate personal preference, of course." And letting her eye fall upon Connors, "For instance, if Kelly here finds a lighter gun for her bra holster, the Agency will pay for it."

Bradley grinned, throwing a glance at the front of Connor's shirt, then replied, "Well, that's good, but I like my 1911." And raising his eyebrows, he added, "That's a .45 and really powerful."

"That's a fun round, Bradley, yes. Somewhat low in velocity, 800 or 900 feet per second. But a lot of mass. The typical round has quite a marked trajectory, but at close range it's awfully affective—

maybe like a bullet train hitting a track walker, yes?"

He stared at her, then simply replied, "Right."

Gretchin reached for her cup, "Be careful, Bradley, she might have you licking the carpet. She know's her weapons, I think."

"Wouldn't want any other gun," he said, ignoring her insult and throwing a look toward Osipov. "It's local."

Coldgrave smiled, then said, "Good for you, Mr. Hopkins. Loyal to the bone, huh? And Ms. Henry, I understand you carry a P-64?" And as Bobbie Lee responded by simply reaching for another pancake, "Watch out for the trigger malfunction. There's a spring in the housing, that slips off. But the nine eighteen cartridge is effective, especially at close range. Hit a man in the chest with that and he'll need a priest. It's a narrow piece. Do you still carry it in your crotch?"

Bobbie Lee blinked, but then answered, "Jesus! You people know ever'thing. Yeah, I carry it in a crotch holster sometimes, except on the bike, which would be rreal stupid."

"Of course, yes. And your rifle is the M44? Very powerful. Let me know if you have any problem getting the ammunition."

"Not so far. I order it online, and it comes in tins. It's great stuff. It's got mercury in it though, so I try not to breathe the smoke too much in practice."

"I understand, yes. And Mr. Osipov, any problem getting the Tokarev ammunition?"

He looked at her hair, then her lips. "Not so far."

"Good," she replied. "Let me know if you do. That's a fast round, makes paper out of body armor." Then, after a sweet sigh, "I have only one other comment about the weapons. Everyone should carry two on the projects. Scandium or whatever, but two. Most of you do now, but please make it the permanent practice of everyone, even for an outing or quick local trip, whenever you leave the premises."

"The Estate," said Maggie.

With a chuckle, "Yes, the Estate, of course."

"So, I guess," said Bradley, "you do know your guns. And what do you carry?"

Gretchin, with a pained expression, said, "Bradley, don't."

"I was just asking."

"Can't you time anything right? Don't you have any class at all?"

He held up both hands. "What? What did I say?"

"Just don't say anything," she shot back. "You're an imbecile. How did you ever get through the Air Force?"

"Boy, you're back to normal, aren't you? Look at you, sitting there with your tattoo and your critical talk." And scowling at her, he pinched up a pancake crumb from his plate and defiantly put it into his mouth.

Coldgrave, clearly ignoring both the question and the bickering, merely took up her cup between gloved finger and thumb.

"Is your point, Mary," asked Martina, "that you don't want us to attempt to make the team more sophisticated?"

"That is correct, Mrs. Osipov. There's a configuration here that must not be deliberately tampered with. Kessler saw it first, then the Agency, and I have seen it, too. No C4, no poison, no electronics. Traditional weapons only. Stick to the rule on this. You can upgrade basic things, weapons, ammunition, even vehicles, if you like. Order what you need through the Agency—call me, I'll get it for you. Or even buy it yourselves and send me the receipts, that's fine. But don't change anything. I like your style. No heroics or moralizing or wondering—just move in, gun them down, and let the blood drip."

A palpable hush followed this, so that Gretchin impulsively gave Bradley an under-the-table kick for staring at the woman. He responded by closing his mouth and looking down at his plate. Martina caught Maggie's look and gave a single blink.

Coldgrave, however, obviously finished with both the breakfast and the conversation, took another sip of coffee and set the cup down upon its holly-and-ivy saucer. Then, as if in preparation for a photo shoot, she opened her mouth half way and with her napkin carefully touched the corners of her lipsticked lips. Ever so elegantly she pushed her chair back and stood.

"And now," she said, "I must be off. Again, thanks to everyone for the wonderful hospitality, including this charming Easter breakfast."

"Christmas," said Maggie.

"Yes, of course, Christmas. Easter's, well, at another time of the year, isn't it? . . . Now, I'll be in touch, everyone. I am so pleased to have met all of you. Maggie, if I may, my coat? We'll see if the Jag turns over."

CHAPTER 19

New Year's Day 2012

"Where is everybody?" queried Gretchin, swaggering into the recreation room. "Hell, it's New Year's Day, for God's sake. Bring out some of the new booze. There's nothing religious about this day—it's parades and sports all day."

Connors, seated beside Bobbie Lee, simply raised her glass of whiskey in acknowledgment, then tipped it toward the uncapped bottle on the table. They, along with Martina and Maggie, sat before the huge TV, whose screen glowed with the flowers, horses, bands, and twirling batons of the Rose Bowl Parade.

"God, what a spectacle!" Gretchin exclaimed softly, falling into a recliner. "What I wouldn't give for some of that sunshine. Look at those people. How'd they end up with California, and me, with Pennsylvania?"

"Aye," said Connors, "and Coldgrave, weth New York. Don't yous feel sorry for her, now."

"Yes," said Maggie, "and she has to go to all those boring parties."

Martina nodded. "And drive there in Jaguar."

Gretchin got up and reached for the bottle and a glass. "Let's not be picking on the lady."

"*Lady* might be the right term," said Bobbie Lee, "but she wears enough lipstick to grease a motorcycle wheel."

Gretchin sat down with her drink. "That's jealousy talking there, I think."

"Well," said Maggie, "I, personally, am jealous of the clothes."

"And," Martina added, "the lipstick may have been thick, but it was gorgeous."

Pointing to the screen, Gretchin put in, "Where'd California get so goddamn many palm trees? It's not Tahiti, and it's not summer."

"So," said Bobbie Lee, burping, "what's ever'body think about our Ms. Coldgrave? Think it's gonna work? What's our team leader here think?"

With a click of her tongue, "I don't know. I kind of like her. I get a good feeling about her actually. She certainly knows her guns."

"The men seem to like her," said Gretchin, beginning to feel the whiskey. "But men are easily impressed. I mean, if she crosses her legs again in front of Bradley, she'll probably give him a hard-on."

"I think," said Maggie, "she's extremely sophisticated and yet has an innocence about her. I like her, too, I think."

Connors nodded. "She's gotta be batter'n Kassler. What a fucker!"

"Yeah," said Bobbie Lee, "that guy was a real outhouse."

Momentarily Gretchin said, "Well, it sounds like we're going to give Mary a fair shot, then."

"Of course," returned Martina.

Toward the end of January the promised packet of info and photos arrived from Coldgrave. But two days after that she called Martina to say that the project had been postponed until the spring. Intel had reported that the targets would probably not attempt to leave the country until June. During this window the team were to come up with a number of plans based on the intel provided. But until the spring, said Coldgrave, everyone could just relax and enjoy the snow.

"Did I hear that right?" Gretchin queried with a scowl. "*Enjoy the snow*, really? That's annoying, honestly."

Martina pushed her salad back. "I don't think she meant anything by it."

"Nothing condescending, huh?"

"It comes with the territory. Managers are like that. I'm like that as team leader."

Pushing a handful of hair behind her ear, "There's a lot of nonsense about this woman I'm just going to have to work past. The glamour stuff's okay, the sexy stuff's okay, but I don't like being talked down to like I'm a goddamn kid. I'm not going to go out an kill people for this lady and have her talk down to me. No way, Martina."

"I don't read her that way."

"Neither do I," agreed Maggie. "Let's just give her a chance."

"You know what?" said Bobbie Lee. "I don't like richies, but I say, let's don't take offence until we have to."

Gretchin cocked her head. "Fine, okay. . . . But what is it with the Agency? They send us one freak after another. Richard, a certifiable psycho. I don't know exactly how he saw us, but it wasn't good. Then Paul. God! He saw us as criminals, admit it."

Connors looked up from her tea. "I'm not a criminal, I'm an assassin."

The Russian breathed a sympathetic sigh. "KGB people were always crazy, it is fact."

Gretchin wrinkled her nose. "I don't care about the KGB, Stanley. . . . Look, people, all I'm saying is, I don't want to be sent out to play in the snow."

"You complain too much, Gretchin," said Bradley. "Just let it go."

In his room, Bradley took the 1911 from its holster and dropped its magazine. Grabbing the oil cloth, he sat down and began to rub the gun's slide. He shouldn't have said it that way. It was pretty stupid, for now she would wait for him with gasoline and torch. But why did she hate him so much? Then he turned, for there was a gentle knock at the door.

Opening, he looked into her face and then said, "Sorry." And when she said nothing, he added, "You hate me, don't you?"

"No. It's just the opposite. . . . I'm in love with you."

He reached out to her, took her by the shoulders, and drew her close. Closing his eyes, he heard her whisper, and from her voice all the usual harshness was gone.

"Let me sleep with you," she said, putting her forehead against his neck. "You're a man, and I need a man."

He frowned and opened his eyes. "But you love me, right?"

"Yes," she replied softly, kissing his neck. "Yes, I do."

Later, as they lay together, he asked, "Gretchin, why are you so mean to me? Why do you do it? Why do you love me and hate me at the same time?"

"I have no idea," she replied, holding him. "I do love you, and I do hate you. What can I say?"

Closing his eyes, "Say what you want, but could you please just be nice to me?"

"I love the way you smell."

He smiled, his eyes still closed. "Yeah?"

"Yeah."

"And I," he said, "love the way you smell."

Wilmington, North Carolina, March

In glaring sunlight the SUV pulled close to the curb across the street from the bank, while from the opposite direction the Corvette moved into a parking place half a block away. Within minutes, the motorcycle rumbled slowly past the SUV, took a right at the corner, and eventually made its way around the block. At the final corner, the motorcycle stopped, then made a right and pulled up just behind the SUV.

"Turn us out," said Connors at the side of Bobbie Lee's helmet.

After angling the bike out to face the bank, Bobbie Lee planted her boots and let the engine idle. "Don't tell me how to ride a motorcycle," she growled over her shoulder, giving the throttle a quick turn.

Connors, keeping her boots on the rests, put her phone to her ear. Momentarily she reported to Bobbie Lee, "She says et won't be long."

"Then git yersilf ready, girl."

"Don't tell me how to kell people."

Inside the SUV, Stanley, his window all the way down and his eyes trained on the front door of the bank, muttered, "I hope these two bull riders do not get killed having their fun. This is ridiculous, I am thinking."

Beside him, Martina, her phone to her ear, replied, "Sure it is." And turning, she could see through the rear window the helmets of the riders as they steadied themselves for the attack.

Connors, hearing this conversation through her phone, said simply, "Tell your husband not to worry."

Martina relayed the message, then spoke into the phone, "It could be any second now, Kelly, they've been in there about five minutes. Just be ready to go."

Connors, keeping the phone to her ear, merely gave a quick sniff at the warning. With her other hand she reached into her jacket, withdrew the magnum from the shoulder rig, and laid it across her lap, up against Bobbie Lee's back. When another warning came, for her to keep her eyes on the bank, she replied into the phone, "Don't tell me how to fuckin' kell people, Martina."

"Fine," Martina came back. "Wait for my confirmation, then go. . . . Any second, I'm guessing."

"Any momant," Connors repeated to Bobbie Lee, "t'en we're a go."

The other nodded, clutching in and tapping into first, her eyes on the bank, her hand on the throttle.

But moments turned into minutes, until everyone's back grew stiff from the tension—everyone's, that is, except Connors'.

Then Bobbie Lee muttered, "Come on, let's go to this here rodeo. Where are they?" But when a woman got out of a car that was parked beside the bank, put a baby in a stroller, and began to push it, she felt her heart race. Only a few other pedestrians could now be seen on the nearby sidewalks, and the car traffic passing by was very light. With a shake of her head, she looked again to the bank doors.

Connors sniffed again, but then said suddenly into her phone, "Et's tham."

Martina, also seeing the targets, said quickley to Connors, "Hold up, wait." Rapidly she scanned the woman and baby and the other foot traffic, then drew a short breath, blew it out, and spoke into her phone, "All right, Kelly, that's a go. Shoot straight."

Pocketing the phone, Connors said at the side of Bobbie Lee's helmet, "Lat's go." And taking up the magnum, she cocked it and held it down to her side.

Bobbie Lee, however, hesitated, for the two men had suddenly halted. Standing with one of the bank doors half open, the two men were apparently engaged in an argument. A moment later, they emerged fully, took a couple of steps, then stopped to face each other, one pointing his finger in the other's face.

Connors said quickly, "Go now."

Letting the clutch out, Bobbie Lee launched them into a slow pace to cross the street. Bouncing them over the curb, she twisted the throttle, molded herself to the tank, and as Connors brought the magnum up ran the motorcycle directly at the men. But one of the men, his eyes enlarging, was already responding and reaching for a weapon. Keeping her eyes steady upon them, Bobbie Lee determined not to flinch from the ferocious blast she knew would come from Connors' gun.

A heartbeat later, before the man could fire, Connors pulled the trigger—*Flam!*—hitting him in the chest and blowing him backward upon the walkway. Instantly she swung from the now veering machine, steadied herself and leveled at the other man, who stood with his mouth open, oddly cringing, as if too rigid to turn away. Deftly she pulled through the double action—*Flam!*— hitting him in the rib cage and spinning him. Then stepping quickly but calmly toward the sprawled men, she put the muzzle at the face of the first, and fired, blowing the eye from its socket. Not bothering to step over to the second man, who lay writhing on his back, she leveled gun and fired at his head. But the Harley had spun its semicircle upon the lawn and was bearing toward her. As she turned to catch it, she saw the face of a woman who had just exited the bank. The woman's expression was one of surprise, but nothing more, even as she stared down at the slain men, one with his eye socket oozing, the other with a quadrant of his skull gone.

As the motorcycle slid to a stop Connors grasped Bobbie Lee's belt, swung up behind her, and found the posts with her boots. Instantly, Bobbie Lee opened the throttle and clutched out, throwing the Harley forward. With it's mighty power plant throwing its exhaust and its rear tire churning up the grass, the Roadster soon flew from the curb and hit the street, and the two women, like wraiths on a roaring white monster, were carried away.

From her seat, Martina watched as the woman with the stroller and the other onlookers, who had all frozen at the ghastly scene, slowly became animated again.

"Tell me," said Stanley, bringing his window up, "just why they had to be doing it this way. It is ridiculous and dangerous. And look at that lawn, it is like a tractor tore it up."

She did not reply, but still surveying the awful scene, she merely pressed two buttons on the phone, put it to her ear and said, "Gretchin, it's done. Drive away. See you at home."

Like choreographed dancers in a horror play, the two vehicles crept from their respective niches, moved away in opposite directions, left the city, and eventually melded with the traffic of the sunny highways.

CHAPTER 20

As the SUV began to make its way west, toward the northbound artery, Martina opened the phone. She pressed two buttons and waited. "Mary? . . . It's done. . . . Yes. . . . Yes, both targets, and no one was with them. Intel was very good. . . . Yes, we're headed out now. . . . Uh, no—no casualties. . . . Okay, talk to you later. . . . Bye." Then she closed the phone, pulled her visor down, and looked into the mirror.

"No casualties," repeated Stanley. "But there could have been casualties—very easily. You did not tell her that part."

"I look tired," she muttered, pushing the visor up. "I feel tired."

"It was a circus."

"Maybe," she replied. "But it was successful."

"And are you going to say the crowd just loved it?"

"No," she answered. "No, I'm not going to say that."

It was an hour later that Bradley dropped his dark glasses onto the console. "Those girls are badass. I mean it—bad *ass*."

"You might want to deemphasize that," replied Gretchin, pushing a handful of hair behind an ear.

"Okay, how about *really* badass."

"That's what they pay them for."

"Yeah, but this is like more, it's like art or something."

She looked at his profile as he drove. His grin of wonder seemed so very simple. "You *are* a child," she said.

Snatching up the glasses and putting them on again, "Don't do that critical stuff, okay? There's nothing I hate more in all this world than your heat. Do you always have to see me as immature?"

She put her head back. "Just get me home, jerkoff."

"Did you see the way that Harley moved? Boy, that Bobbie Lee can ride."

"Well, I just hope they don't get themselves killed."

"Hey," he returned, "getting killed on a Harley is considered an honor."

Throwing up a hand, "Great. I'm impressed."

Then he queried, "Want to stop somewhere for the night?"

"No."

"We could get some wine, drink it in bed."

"No, thanks."

"We could take a shower together."

"If you say that again," she said wearily, "I'm going to hit you so goddamn hard you'll swallow your side teeth."

"You're just being mean again."

"Try me, asshole."

"But what about love?"

"Never heard of it."

"I know you," he said. "I know your sadistic side. I understand you, Gretchin. You like sex, you like love, but you have to be a badass yourself. Otherwise, you don't feel you're alive. I understand."

"Careful, buddy, you're gonna need a dentist, I'm warning you. Just keep driving and get me home. . . . I hope we can stop for dinner, maybe twice. I hate long rides."

He took the glasses off again. "Sure."

"And drive smooth."

"No shower, huh?"

"Careful, my fist is on a hair trigger."

He chuckled. "Whoa, I'm scared. Guess I wouldn't retaliate by blowing your head out the glass with my .45."

Adjusting her position and closing her eyes to rest, she replied, "Not if you loved me, Bradley, not if you loved me."

"Gotcha."

Toward the end of the afternoon, Stanley moved his hands down the steering wheel and queried, "Where would you like to stop for dinner?"

"What?"

"Where do you want to eat? Do you want to stop or just keep driving."

"I don't know."

"I am not tired," he offered, "we can just go on, if you want to."

"No, you *are* tired, you must be. Yes, let's stop."

"But where?"

"I have no idea."

Returning his hands to the top of the wheel, "Well, then, I will choose the place, whatever looks to be good. I am hungry."

"Yes," she returned, "yes, stop somewhere. That would be good." Then momentarily she said, "Do you know what I've been thinking about?"

"No."

"About how you came to me on that first Christmas. It was very cold, and I pulled you inside quickly, and then you stood there holding your gift for me."

"It was New Year's Eve."

"But it was Christmas time. You just stood there. You were staring at my hair."

"Yes. And your eyes, your face. I think I could not move."

She smiled. "That was a very romantic evening, the most romantic of my life. And later you kissed me, right there in the restaurant."

"You asked me to."

"Driving away from everything later was surreal, wasn't it?"

"We were lucky."

"Do you wish now that we had driven away forever?"

With a shrug, "I am not sure how to answer. Kessler called you, the Agency apologized, you agreed to work for them again, and I agreed to work with you. It is all very simple. And I am supposed to be wishing something else?"

"Are you still in love with me?"

Wondering why she should be asking this, he replied, "Even more now."

She smiled again. "And I with you, Mr. Osipov—and I with you."

"And this is an accomplishment, you are thinking?"

"It is more than that," she replied, "it is defying gravity."

When the idling engine had rumbled to a stop, Bobbie Lee extracted the key and pushed it into an outside pocket of her road jacket. Removing her helmet, she squeezed her eyes shut, blinked, puffed her cheeks, and looked up at the evening stars.

Connors, who had gotten off and was stretching, watched her. "What're you lookin' at?"

"Somethin' with a lot of eyes."

"T'ink et's lookin' at you?"

Replying with a shake of her head, Bobbie Lee watched as Connors lifted her helmet, smoothed her hair, then ran a hand down the front of her jacket. "That's right, you've got meat all over you, and you've rubbed it all over my back. You shot that boy in the eye. It prob'ly landed in yer pocket, you oughta check. Guess you liked havin' a magnum today." Then she swung her leg off, snapped her chinstrap, and let the helmet dangle from her fingers.

"Guess I ded," was the reply.

"Good of Packard to loan it."

"Guess et was."

"You should thank him."

"Guess I will."

"Well, girl, I hope you had fun. I don't think I can hear anymore, and I think you burned my helmet. It was worse in Texas though, you almost set my hair on fire."

As the two stood looking up at the stars, a semi truck rolled slowly past them, then another, then a third, grumbling toward the big parking spots, where truckers might catch some sleep.

Bobbie Lee unzipped her sleeves. "Food? And you better git some coffee in you, or you'll fall off the back of this here motorcycle."

"Nah, I've got a grep on you."

As they came to the double doors, they stopped briefly to look up again at the sky.

"Some women," said Bobbie Lee, pulling one of the doors open, "come out to truck stops like this lookin' for men."

With a grimace, "They're shetheads."

"The truckers?"

"The women."

"Maybe they need it."

"Sounds loike you do."

Bobbie Lee gave her helmet a playful swing. "Nope."

Following a visit to the restroom, where they also wiped their jackets down with paper towels, they ordered a pizza and took seats at a table to wait.

"Ef you don't need et," said Connors, plopping her helmet onto the table, "what do you need?"

With a raise of the eyebrows, "I think I need love actually. Sex is pritty cheap, but love costs the whole goddamn world. ... I don't think I need marriage, that's fer sure. That can be one hell of a nasty situation, and it's not too easy to git out of, neither."

"So I've haerd."

"I'm supposed to need men, but I don't think I do. My Gramma used to say there wasn't nothin like a good man on a cold night."

"What do *you* say?"

A shrug. "Who cares? Besides, with all this talk about same-sex marriage, I jist might put in to marry my motorcycle."

"So, you're not lookin'?"

Another shrug. "I'm okay bein' alone."

Stretching out her legs, Connors ran a hand through her hair. "You can't joost keep sleepin' weth a bottle of wheskey and a gun."

"You're tellin' *me* this?"

Crossing her legs and looking at her boots, as if to inspect them, "I'm not tellin' you anyt'ing."

"Yeah, you ain't and you are at the same time, girl. 'Sides, we're talkin' about two different things here, a man and marriage, two different things completely. Not sure I want either actually. ... Where's that pizza?"

"Et's only been ten minutes."

"Well, let's git to cookin', people. I've been turnin' a throttle all day, which is harder than pullin' a trigger, I can tellya."

When the guttural chuckling of two men at a nearby table grew louder, Bobbie Lee turned to get a look at them. She took in their jeans, T-shirts, ball caps, and their grimy fingers drumming impatiently upon the table. Apparently they too were waiting for their order.

One of them, catching her look, said, "We've been list'nin' to you two girls over here, and now we know all about you. Why don't you come over here and talk to us?"

She did not look away, but continued to eye them. Connors simply ignored them.

"Come over here, baby," the other said. "I need it like you need it. Drivin' a rig ain't no fun, not like you'd be."

Without looking at them, Connors muttered audibly, "I wesh t'is stuff dedn't happen. Et seems to happen frequently."

Turning back from them, Bobbie Lee replied, "That's 'cause you're a glamour girl, prob'ly, which gives you the pick of the litter. It doesn't happen to me all that much—maybe because of my muscles. But it's pritty distasteful when it does happen. Sometimes it makes me downright mad." Throwing them a glance, she added, "Lord, look at them dirty fingers. I'll bet those two're dirty all over."

"Bat they are, too."

The first one spoke again. "We're waiting over here. I've got the urge."

Without looking at them, Bobbie Lee said with a sigh, "Now it's gonna git raucous, I guess. They're startin' to be a menace."

Then he said, "I can smell you all the way over here, and I don't mean your perfume."

"Maybe," she continued, "I should go over and kick their ass."

Connors threw them a glance. "They look beefy, to me."

A shrug. "More ass to kick."

"What about me pizza?"

"They're a menace. And they're goddamn annoying, if you ask me."

"Maybe et's joost freedom of speech."

"Maybe it's harassment."

Connors rolled her eyes. "Ignore 'am. You'll survoive."

"I never take my survival as a given."

"You can't do much about t'is kind of harassment anyway."

After taking her watch off and laying it face up on the table, Bobbie Lee said softly, "I'll betcha I can knock the front teeth outta both of them with my pistol—an' I won't fire a shot, not one—an' have 'em on the floor a-screamin' in less than half a minute. Betcha a goddamn nickel, what d'you say? Come on, take me up on it, girl. There's the watch, you can time me. Don't be cheap, now, what's a nickel?"

Connors took another look at them, then pushed the watch back. "The pizza's about ready, ours is naxt."

Another teasing call. "I've got somethin' under the table here for you girls."

With obvious disappointment, Bobbie Lee strapped on her watch, then answered him, "We don't really wanna see what you've got, boys, we're doin' all right over here."

"Come have a stinky look," he taunted, and when there was no response, "You girls look like biker chicks. You ain't gonna put none of your biker violence on us, are you?"

"No," she answered, "we don't believe in violence, we believe in love."

"Whoa," he exclaimed with a laugh. "Love. That's what I want right now. Come over here, biker chicks, and give us some love." When both women ignored this, he said, "You look like alligators, to me, a couple of snake chicks right outta hell."

Then Connors turned to them. attempted a smile, and said, "We don't believe in violence, we're peaceful."

With a grunt, "I'll betcha are. But I'll betcha need it where it counts, too. Come on over."

"No," she replied, turning from them, "we're doin' joost foine roight here."

www.ingramcontent.com/pod-product-compliance
Lightning Source LLC
Chambersburg PA
CBHW071556110726
47908CB00007B/2128